BODY TO DIE FOR

D.J. Swiger

I dedicate this book to my family, my friends and my beloved dog Jessie

Acknowledgments

I'm so thankful to my editor Colleen Ezzell who was not only encouraging to me, but also very patient. I'd also like to thank my lovely friends and Beta readers Beth May, Keitha Jenkins, Deonne Lohrenz, Ellen Croom and Lisa Rigsbee. I'm blessed to have such good friends who are willing to take the time to not only read my manuscript, but to offer constructive criticism. Last but not least, I'd like to thank my husband, Phil, for putting up with me and my grumpiness when I struggled with writer's block and was willing to give it all up. He kept me going.

Contents

Chapter 1

Monica Gallagher trudged up the 37 steps that led to Newport Yoga and Pilates studio. Most days she raced up the stairs, trying to get to her early morning class before the first students arrived. This morning, however, things were different. The night before, the studio had thrown a big party in honor of its third anniversary. There was food catered by Mother's Market, wine from the small neighborhood wine shop and at about 9:30 one of the yoga teachers put on some oldies and everyone started to dance. Monica was one of the last to leave after enjoying a heady flirtation with one of her few male clients.

Monica tried to be in bed no later than 10:30. Most days she was scheduled to teach the early morning crowd and she needed her sleep. The previous late night made the hike up the steep stairs that much more difficult. She had a busy morning ahead of her and she hoped she could get through it without losing her patience; fatigue took a toll on her patience.

She got to the top of the stairs and pulled out her key. She could see that the reception area had not been completely cleared up by the cleaning crew, which made her think that maybe they cut corners due to the late hour.

1

There were a few plates on the reception desk and three red balloons floating in the air. She grabbed the plates, tossed them in the garbage and then hurried back to the studio at the end of the hallway. The front section of the studio consisted of two classrooms, which were used mostly for yoga and a few Pilates mat classes. She had ten minutes before her first client was scheduled to arrive and Monica liked having the time to get things ready in the studio and to mentally prepare for the day.

As she walked down the hallway toward the studio, Monica noticed that the studio really could use a good cleaning. She was surprised that the cleaning crew, who were scheduled to come after the party was over, had done such a lousy job. Had they even shown up? She made a mental note to let Jessica, the office manager, know that things were out of kilter. Newport Beach was not the type of place that would support anything even remotely out of order.

As she entered the studio, Monica noticed two plastic cups half full of wine placed upright on the Cadillac table. Beneath her feet she felt a sticky substance, which she assumed was spilled white wine. She picked up the glasses in one hand and walked over to the small garbage pail by the desk. Dropping the cups in the garbage, she made a face. How disgusting, she thought. Who would be so sloppy as to leave the studio looking like a cheap bar? Monica sighed and tossed her handbag onto the chair near the desk. Her first client was difficult; She was never happy, never said thank you and sometimes made snide remarks about Monica's fitness wardrobe. She needed to take a few deep breaths and let it go.

As Monica headed over to the closest reformer, she froze. Next to the reformer bed lay a body. Monica immediately recognized her as a regular at the studio and someone who had been at the open house the previous night. Monica thought about touching her to see if she was still alive and to determine whether she could use some of those CPR and lifesaving skills she had learned throughout the years. But it was obvious that no amount of mouth-to-mouth could save this woman; she was dead and had been for quite a while. Monica began to scream but quickly collected herself and picked up her phone to call 911.

Chapter 2

The police were there within minutes, although it seemed much longer to Monica. The distressed Pilates instructor was told to leave the facility immediately and to wait for the police outside. She was seated at the bottom of the steps shaking and crying after what she had discovered, but she managed to text her morning client to let her know that her session was cancelled. Additional information would be sent later.

She could hear the sirens almost as soon as she hung up the phone, but it could be anything at this hour of the morning. Traffic accidents were a daily occurrence from dawn until long past dusk. With so many freeways and so many people, someone was bound to crash. But right now, as she sat shaking at the bottom of the staircase, all she could think about was that dead woman.

Monica took a deep breath, knowing at least she was safe outside. People were parking their cars in the lot just outside the studio getting ready for the workday. Several people glanced her way wondering what was going on, but no one walked over to her. She was glad, as she had no desire to retell the story, at least not until the emergency vehicles arrived. She realized that the smart thing to do at this point would be to call Jessica Howard, the office manager, and let her know what happened. Sooner or later someone would be contacting Jessica, and it made more sense if Monica made the call. She realized that Jessica may be trying to sleep in after the long night but, if anything was worth waking her up, this was. She tucked behind her ear a loose lock of hair that had fallen out of her messy bun and dialed Jessica's number. As Monica expected, a very sleepy voice answered. "Hello," Jessica said, sounding still very much asleep. "Monica? Is that you?"

Monica tried hard to keep the tears out of her voice and had to breathe deeply before being able to speak. "Jess," she said losing it completely. "It's bad here. Something bad has happened." At this point the first police car pulled in and the sound of the siren could be heard on the other end of the phone. "I can't talk now. You need to be here." She hung up. She tried to stand up and walk over to the police vehicle, but fear paralyzed her. Seeing the officers made the situation seem that much more real. Until that time, part of her believed it was just a bad dream and she was still sound asleep waiting for the alarm to go off. Two male officers stepped out of the car while a second car and an ambulance pulled in next to them. The two officers, who looked to be in their late 30s or early 40s, walked over to the stairs. She looked up, her face a mess of tears.

"Are you the one who called this in?" asked the taller of the two men. The other officer hovered behind him. "Your name is Monica Gallagher?" She nodded, still unable to speak. The shorter officer came up and offered her a hand to help her stand up. She took his hand, and with some effort got to her feet. She wiped the tears from her face.

"Monica," said the taller officer. "I need you to stay here. We're going up to the studio to see if it's safe. We'll need to ask you a few questions when we return, so please don't go anywhere." Monica nodded as she wiped the tears from her eyes. "Please let the paramedics know if you need any assistance. They can help you out if needed." The two officers proceeded up the stairs, their hands on their guns. A couple of paramedics carrying a stretcher and a large bag followed behind. "You need help?" asked one of them. Monica shook her head. Other than a strong tranquilizer, there wasn't much that would help her.

She stayed by the steps and another car pulled up. This time it was a woman who climbed out of the car and walked over to her. In the meantime, everyone out in the parking lot was rubbernecking to see what was happening. Some got in their cars and left, sensing that it was not a safe place to be.

"Monica," said the female officer. "My name is Officer Green and we need you stay here as we check the facility to make sure no one is still there. I'll be staying here with you," she said in a comforting manner. "Do you mind if I ask you a few questions while the other officers are up in the facility checking it out?"

"No, I don't mind," Monica said. The officer lowered herself onto the step next to her and Monica waited for her to speak. The officer's presence felt reassuring. "It's okay if you ask me questions," she repeated, finding her voice. "I can't say much because once I saw the – um – body I called 911 and left. I never saw anyone else."

"That's okay Monica. You did the right thing. That should have been what the 911 operator advised you to do so yeah, you did the right thing." Monica nodded.

"What will happen now," said Officer Green. "is that there will be a detective or two assigned to this case and they'll be asking you more questions. Don't worry about it and just answer them to the best of your ability. They'll be here soon."

At that point Jessica Howard arrived at the scene. She was dressed in a pair of black yoga pants and a long green top, with her long blonde hair tied into a high ponytail. Other than a light sweep of pink lip gloss, she was make-up free.

"Officer," she called as she raced from her car to the building entrance, "I am the manager here and I got here as soon as I could." She extended her hand to the female officer who remained seated next to the frightened instructor. "My name is Jessica Howard and like I said, I got here as soon as I could."

The officer explained to the manager that she would be required to stick around and answer questions once the detective team showed up. It was routine in a murder investigation, she said. She also suggested that Jessica contact as many clients and students as possible to let them know that the studio was closed. "Handle it any way you see fit," said Officer Green. "But you need to let your clients know, and it would be best if people didn't show up while the initial investigation is going on."

7

"Of course," said the manager, pulling her phone out of her purse, not sure where to begin. She would hang out here for as long as needed to direct away anyone who showed up for the earlier morning classes. She realized that down the road this would turn into a true damage control nightmare. She shivered at the thought. "I'll take care of it now."

"Good," said Officer Green, standing up and wiping some dust of her uniform pants. "I'm sure you will."

"Does Monica need to stay?" Jessica asked as she held the phone up to her ear.

"Just until the detective team shows up," the officer glanced at her watch. "It should be any minute. It won't take long, and they can always call her later if needed."

Jessica called three of the instructors to explain the situation and to have them get started on calling their clients scheduled for that day. She also called the scheduling service to have the class marked as cancelled for anyone who planned to sign up at the last minute. She then browsed the Pilates room schedule to see who was scheduled in the morning. She saw that Monica had three clients in a row. "Monica?" she asked gently. "Could you contact all of the clients you had scheduled this morning and cancel them?" Monica agreed and searched her phone for the contact info.

Just as the instructor reached her client by phone, a sedan pulled in and two men stepped out. One was tall and stocky and the other was also tall, but younger and well built. The younger detective had sandy colored hair and striking green eyes. They were dressed in plain clothes with blazers, and the older detective wore a necktie. They walked toward the scene and Officer Green whispered that they were the detectives. "They'll take over from here." Monica nodded while Jessica who was still on the phone held her hand up in a gesture to indicate that they should wait. The detectives approached the two women and waited for them to finish their calls. The older of the two had dark, close cropped hair and his face was lightly tanned as if he had spent some time in the sun.

"Hello there," the older detective extended his hand to Jessica. "I am Detective James Mahoney, and this is my partner Detective Martin Sanders. We've been assigned this case and after we talk to the officers up there," he pointed to the top of the stairs, "we're going to have to ask you a series of questions. We also need to make sure that your clientele is aware of the situation and that you or someone will do what's necessary to inform them. For the immediate future, this facility will be under investigation." He looked directly at Jessica. "Have you already called or tried to call anyone expected to come in today to let them know that the studio is closed?" Jessica nodded and pointed to Monica who was on the phone with someone. "Between the two of us we'll get this done," she replied. He nodded and looked back at his notes.

"It is also our understanding that someone by the name of Monica Gallagher was the one who discovered the body inside the building." He looked around. "Is Monica here?"

"Yes," said Jessica pointing in Monica's direction. She had her back to them, and the phone pressed tightly to her ear. "That's Monica. I had her contact all her morning clients to let them know that the studio was closed due to an emergency." The detective nodded again and said nothing.

"We will need to question her," he added pointing his chin toward Monica. "Once she is done calling everyone, we all need to get together and discuss what we know."

"Yes, of course," Jessica agreed.

At that moment, Monica slipped the phone into her jacket pocket and walked toward the group gathered at the bottom of the stairs. She looked calmer than she had earlier and ready to talk. Jessica took the lead.

"Monica. These are detectives Mahoney and Sanders, and they need to talk to us for a little while to try to make some sense of what happened. They're asking us to stick around a bit longer to answer some questions."

"Is that okay?" This was Sanders speaking for the first time and Jessica noticed that he had a kind face; she found him appealing in rugged masculine way.

"I don't mind. I was the one who found her so I would probably be the best person to answer questions."

Just then the first responders came down the stairs carrying the body on a stretcher. She was covered in a zippered bag. The sight of the body on the stretcher shocked Monica and she turned away. The detectives excused themselves and walked over to the police officers who were now huddled in a circle. Both detectives lowered their heads as they listened intently to the officers while writing furiously in their notebooks.

"I wonder what they found," Monica asked, sounding nervous once again.

Jessica shrugged. "I guess we'll find out," she said. "Trust me, we'll be actively involved in this whether or not we want to be." Monica did not look pleased and she stepped away from her boss.

"In the meantime," added Jessica as she pushed behind her ear a strand of hair that had come loose from her ponytail, "stay close." She then walked over to the officers and detectives who were speaking in low voices.

"Everything has been cleared in the studio. The officers checked to make sure, so would it be okay if we go up together?" said Mahoney.

"Or course," said Jessica as she started up the stairs. "Follow me."

The two women, along with the two detectives, walked up the steep stairwell. Jessica thought to herself from now on it would never be the same. This high-end yoga/Pilates studio in a fashionable section of Newport Beach would always have the stigma of being a murder site. The thought gave her a chill. This would either make or break the studio as some people, even in affluent Orange County, got a thrill out of this sort of thing. Whether or not they would continue to take classes was another story altogether.

As the group walked into the main area, Detective Mahoney was winded from the 37 steps. He entered the reception area and wiped a bead of sweat off his forehead. It was not hot outside, but his body was clearly out of shape. Jessica offered the two detectives chairs, which she pulled out of the back room. "Is this okay?" she asked, pointing to two metal chairs. "I can go grab a bolster or a pillow to make them more comfortable, if you'd like," she offered. The detectives shook their heads.

"Just as an update, the victim was strangled. It appears that the culprit strangled her and then wiped away any evidence. We don't yet have the time of death, but it appears to have been very late last night." Detective Mahoney cleared his throat and continued. "We also know that there was a party going on last night so it must have happened shortly after everyone – or almost everyone – went home. We'll need a list of everyone who attended the party."

"Of course, officer," said Jessica, doing her best to stay calm. The idea of someone being strangled in the Pilates studio was terrifying. She tried to think of just about anything else as she continued. "We can't emphasize enough how difficult this is for us. The victim was a client of ours." She looked over at the Pilates teacher who was looking at no one in particular. Jessica continued. "Monica recognized her from some of her mat classes. Rebekah King had been a member here for some time and she did both Pilates and yoga on a regular basis," the young manager said as she crossed and uncrossed her legs. The seat was becoming uncomfortable and even in the best of circumstances she was not accustomed to sitting this long. "Rebekah was a lovely lady. Everyone liked her and..."

"And?"

"Well, as you can imagine here in Newport Beach, a lot of people are very wealthy and privileged, and they tend to want things their own way. If they don't like a new teacher, they let us know. If a class turns out to be less challenging than they expected, again they let us know. Rebekah – um – the victim never was like that. She was always happy and rarely cancelled her sessions. When she had to cancel due to whatever circumstance, she never bitched about being charged for a late cancellation. She was very easy to deal with." Monica nodded in agreement to what her boss was saying but remained silent.

Again, Detective Mahoney nodded and wrote in his pad. Detective Sanders glanced at Jessica and she took notice. He was a very attractive and exactly her type. He also had a thick gold band around his ring finger.

"Do you think there may have been someone here at the studio who had a problem with the victim? I know you said she was easy to work with and rarely complained, but maybe there was someone on your staff that she didn't get along with?" Detective Sanders asked.

"Not that I am aware of," Jessica answered without giving it much thought. Was it possible someone didn't get along with her? This was a highly competitive city and there were plenty of resentments to go around. She needed to ask around to see if anyone on her staff was aware of any bad blood between the victim and another student.

"Tell us about the anniversary party last night." Detective Mahoney said without looking up from his notes. "I think you told me that she was here."

'Yes, I believe she was," Jessica replied. "I remember seeing her in the studio with a few of the teachers drinking wine and having a good time. She was wearing a really cute dress and I remember telling her how nice she looked. You rarely see students in anything other than yoga pants and sports bras so when they look good, you notice it." Both detectives nodded but neither took notes.

13

"Did she seem at all distressed? Was she there with anyone? Do you know anything at all about her marriage or her love life?"

The questions continued and Jessica did her best to answer them, but she was getting tired and felt she needed a break. There was so much to do now, and she still had the company to manage one way or another.

At that point, a tall good-looking young man walked into the studio. He had thick dark hair and olive skin. He was lean and muscular with sculpted features and clear blue eyes. Even the two detectives took notice. He was wearing a light brown leather jacket and a pair of old faded jeans. "Jess!" he called. "What is going on here? I got a call that something happened last night, and I got over here as soon as I could." The young man looked visibly upset. "I can't believe there has been a murder here. A murder! I just saw it on the local news station." His movie-star good-looks faded momentarily and he looked as if he could cry. Detective Sanders took note of the newcomer's distress. Either this was one of many young actor wannabes populating the area or he was seriously upset about something. He engaged in a private and somewhat agitated conversation with the office manager, but other than a simple nod, the young man completely ignored the two detectives.

"She was here last night," he said as he paced the room. "We spoke for a few minutes. Shit, we even made a toast to three more years here at NYP. She seemed to be in such a great mood. How could this even happen?"

"Officers. This is Declan Stevens from our yoga staff. He's been here since we opened exactly three years ago and has a great reputation among our members." Stevens smiled and seemed to be pleased by the compliment. "I'm glad you're here," she added. These officers – I mean – detectives have a lot of questions and you can help me answer them." She raised a single brow at the tall newcomer.

Declan Stevens looked both upset and tired. It seemed to the two detectives that everyone in this room was tired due to the party the night before. They were sure that none of them were thrilled at being awakened so early. Declan took a seat on the floor next to Jessica and waved her away when she suggested she get another chair. "I'm good on the floor," he said.

"The detectives need to know anything you might know about Rebekah King. I know she took some of your yoga classes." Detective Mahoney took over. "Was there anything at all you noticed about her over the past few days or maybe her interactions with someone at the studio? Did she seem distressed at all, especially last night? The male yoga teacher listened intently and cocked his head to one side, trying to remember anything that might be of importance.

"I really can't say much. She always seemed nice and she loved yoga and showed up for almost all of my classes. I think," he added looking over at Jessica for confirmation. "She took classes from a few other teachers who did more morning classes and I guess she liked Pilates too," he said pointing towards Monica. "She was a big fan of our studio."

"Can you think of anything else that may be of importance in this investigation?" Sanders asked the entire group. No one said anything. "You understand there is still I a lot we don't know, but we will be talking to each and every one of you very soon." The manager nodded and the detectives closed their notebooks and stood up.

Detective Mahoney checked his watch and signaled to his partner that it was time to leave. "We are heading back to the office and starting to look into matters. Make sure to get in touch with everyone who was at the event last night." Jessica nodded.

"We will be in touch," said Mahoney as they walked out the door.

Chapter 3

Two hours later nearly every member of Newport Beach Yoga and Pilates had been informed of the murder. Of course, it had to be spun in a way that didn't scare people away, but they knew that the studio would be closed for a few days. Jessica Howard, the manager, was learning that she could be remarkably good at spinning disturbing events and turning them into something a little more digestible to the public. She had no idea she had this skill because in the past, she had never experienced anything remotely like this. Most of her life, up until now, had not held much in the way of surprises.

Jessica, who preferred to be called Jess, came from Newport Beach royalty. In other words, money was never a problem. Her father, Walter Howard, was the owner of a large luxury car dealership on Pacific Coast highway and her mother was a highly paid model much in demand once upon a time. Jessica made a valiant attempt to tone down her status as a trust fund baby by driving a late model Honda, mixing Target brand clothes with her Nordstrom's wardrobe and balking at prices at high-end restaurants when dining with friends. The yoga crowd was not impressed by money or the ability to have pretty much anything one's heart desired. At least that's what they preached. But many of them drove up to the studio in BMWs and Mercedes wearing $100 Lululemon yoga pants. It was all a matter of perception, and Jessica was good at the game.

Now she was trying to make sense of what happened. A murder! Someone was killed in her studio! She had to provide a list of all the members from the past two years. Apparently, the confidentiality agreement had to be broken when it came to murder, so she reluctantly handed over the list. Nowhere in any of the operation materials was this fact noted.

The owners of the studio were two wealthy gay men who lived in Brentwood, an affluent Los Angeles neighborhood. They owned several studios throughout the area with a new one scheduled to open soon in Seattle. They were vacationing in St. Bart's and their staff was told to contact them only in a dire emergency. This was without a doubt a *dire emergency*, so Jess picked up her phone and called Spencer – the more agreeable of the two -- to let him know what was going on. She dreaded the call, but it was something she had to do; they were going to find out about it one way or another. Jake, Spencer's husband and co-owner of Newport Beach Yoga and Pilates, didn't much care for her, but she had come to terms with that and when given the choice, she spoke to Spencer.

The call went to voicemail and she figured there was probably a few hours' time difference and they were out snorkeling or scuba diving. She left a message for Spencer to call her back as soon as possible. She left out the details.

After the detectives had left and she had insisted that Monica go back to her apartment and take a day or two to get over the shock, Jessica went home to clean up. She had rushed out of her condo so fast that morning that she hadn't put on any make-up or brushed her hair and she also needed a shower. Detective Sanders, the good-looking one, had contacted her saying that they would need to talk to her at the precinct. She made a mental note to call him back to set that up.

Jessica made the decision to shut down the studio for at least another day to make sure that everything that needed to be done had been done and to give the cleaning crew the entire day to clean up. Fortunately, there was no blood, so the cleanup was relatively simple, but it was almost as if the entire studio needed to be disinfected after the terrible deed. She was also concerned about why the cleaning help had not shown up late last night as expected. She'd have to look into that later. In the meantime, she just needed to get in touch with the owners to let them know what was going on. They were hands off in the management of the studio for the most part and Jess handled all day-to-day problems, but this was more than a problem.

Jessica tried to remember everything she could about Rebekah King to see if there was something unusual or irregular about her that would make someone want to kill her. Of course, no one she knew at the studio was capable of plotting a murder, much less committing one, but these were the types of questions she would be asked.

Detective Mahoney asked her a lot of questions regarding the victim, but she didn't have much to offer.

Most of the clients were wealthy, they had a lot of free time on their hands, and they were nice enough when at the studio. She kept a professional distance from everyone, but other than a handful of unhappy clients, most were very pleasant. Many were divorced and available or divorced and recently remarried. Many were having affairs; some were in happy marriages and all of them needed a diversion like yoga or Pilates. Jessica noticed that those who normally took group yoga classes stuck with yoga and rarely tried the equipment-based Pilates. Then those who were addicted to working in the Pilates studio on equipment were rarely seen in a group yoga class. Rebekah, however, did both, which made her a little different, but it wasn't all that unusual to enjoy both forms of exercise.

Rebekah King was a slender woman in her 40s. She had wavy blonde hair that fell to her shoulders when it wasn't pulled into a ponytail. Her skin was smooth and well cared for with expensive products and facials, and with her toned body she could easily pass for a woman of 35. She seemed friendly enough and never complained about teachers or class size. In Jessica's experienced opinion, she was one of the easier clients. Many of the women who attended classes were friendly and easygoing, but they kept a distance from the staff. Few of them knew who her parents were; otherwise, they would make more of an effort getting to know her. These were the people who dined regularly at Mastro's in Crystal Cove and shopped at the high-end stores in Southcoast Plaza. They took European river cruises once a year and spent Christmas in New York City. When they told her about their visits to New York after the first of the year,

Jessica didn't let on that her father owned a pied-a-terre on 55th and 6th Ave. She spent many a weekend during her New England college years at this two-bedroom flat. There was no need for anyone to ever know.

Other than Rebekah being a wealthy woman with a great body and lovely smile, there was nothing extraordinary about her. Jessica reviewed her file and saw that she consistently took three yoga classes a week when she was in town and two private Pilates class a week with Kim Parker. She made a note to give Kim a call to see if she had any information that might come in handy. As she started for the kitchen to pour herself a glass of cold water, her cell phone rang. She saw from the caller ID that it was Spencer returning her call. She let it ring a few times before picking up. She thought it would be easy to let him know and he may already know as CNN had picked up the story. Then again, knowing them they were probably at the beach all day and she would have the misfortune of having to break the news.

"Spencer," she said as she picked up the phone. Handling angry clients, difficult instructors and pissed-off owners was a skill she had developed over the years and ultimately what had allowed her to keep her job. Three years at a trendy Newport Beach yoga/Pilates studio was a long time for anyone. These were not easy people. Yet she kept her calm and was able to handle just about anything. This, however, was different. "I'm not sure you heard the news but..."

"Of course, I've heard the news. Jake and I came back from a dive and it's all over CNN. What the fuck is going on

Jess? Who gets murdered in a yoga studio? This can't look good for us." Jessica sighed and realized that this crisis management scenario would not be easy. She continued on to the kitchen, opened the fridge and stared at the unopened bottle of Chardonnay. It was too early for wine, but it was tempting. It would have been easier if he first got the news from her. He was clearly upset and when he got angry or upset, his voice rose an octave.

"Spencer, the way we look can be dealt with later. Right now, we have a murder investigation going on and I have to be in charge here. It happened last night after our anniversary bash and it must have happened after we locked up." She shut the refrigerator and walked toward her bedroom. "I was the last to leave. It was around midnight, and the parking lot was nearly empty. As a matter of fact, I'm pretty sure I was the last to leave."

"So whoever it was must have had a key, right? I mean how else could he get in?" She could hear the television blasting in the background with a reporter talking about bad weather heading for the Southeastern U.S. She could visualize Jake sitting on the bed, sipping a martini while his partner managed the business. Even when things were normal enough and did not involve dead bodies in the Pilates studio, Spencer handled the bulk of the business. Pretty boy Jake showed up and mingled with the students and clients from time to time, always feigning a keen interest in what was going on.

"Maybe," replied Jessica twirling a strand of long blonde hair in her fingers. "You never know. These days keys can be copied, and people don't think twice about handing their own sets over to someone else." A wave of nausea hit her like a ton of bricks. She recalled a time when she loaned her own key to a regular student to go back upstairs to get a cell phone that she had left behind after a grueling level three yoga class. At the time she didn't give it much thought as most of the clientele at the studio were not the type to steal or murder. Yet now it seemed like she had done the wrong thing and she wondered who else might be willing to offer a spare key to someone who needed to use the restroom in a pinch. She also had to remember to call the cleaning crew to see what happened to them last night. There was no evidence that they had ever been there. Could they have seen something and left? She made a mental note to call them right away.

"Jake and I will try our best to get home early, but you know how the flights are this time of year. May be difficult to arrange anything so last minute, not to mention the news is saying a storm is on the way, but we will keep you posted. In the meantime, Jess darling, we have a couple's massage scheduled for 15 minutes so I need to get a quick splash in the shower getting all this sea water off me. I'll touch base later, love."

Jessica hung up the phone and rolled her eyes. There was no way that the two lovebirds would schedule an earlier flight. They would continue to prance about St. Bart's hobnobbing with the rich and famous while she buckled down to manage this crisis. Despite having several successful yoga/Pilates studios, the two owners rarely did much of anything to help with the day-to-day business. This situation, she realized, was going to be all on her.

Chapter 4

Detectives Mahoney and Sanders stopped by a small coffee shop before heading back to the precinct. The younger detective had been trying to tempt his partner into drinking expensive coffee with the texture and color of tar. Mahoney, who was just old enough to remember the days when a cup of American coffee was as transparent as tea, ordered his daily cup anyway, along with a sugary pastry.

"You really should try the cappuccino," said Sanders stirring his tall drink with a stick. "It's really good and you wouldn't need to order that," he said pointing to a three-layer pastry with a strawberry topping.

"Nah, that's okay. I just spent $8.55 getting what I could get over at Albertson's for less than half that, so I am guessing that all of this pricey stuff has to work miracles. "His partner laughed and took a careful sip of his hot coffee. There was a crowd of younger people in the coffee shop staring at their phones or typing wildly on their laptops. It was 11 a.m., a time when most young people should be at work. Newport Beach, although technically not Los Angeles, was still considered to be in the greater Los Angeles area and there were many screenwriter and actor wannabees holding down service jobs until they got their big break. It was an unusually attractive crowd in the coffee shop this morning, with everyone within five pounds of their ideal body weight and facial features that could hold their own next to any celebrity. Mahoney looked around and instinctively sucked in his gut. He was up to 217 pounds, which was, as his wife reminded him on a daily basis, at least 20 pounds over his ideal weight. He liked the sweets too much and kale just didn't do it for him.

"So what's your take on all this?" he asked, taking a big bite out of his pastry. "This looks more like something out of Law and Order SVU than something that would take place here in Newport Beach. I didn't think rich people killed each other all that often."

"You know better than that, James. Rich people kill each other all the time but the stories are far more romantic. Usually there is a sexual side to the story involving some rich businessman and his 16-year-old girlfriend. Do you remember the doctor who went around drugging young girls and raping them?" Mahoney nodded. That particular case was a huge sensation as the doctor was young, good-looking and wealthy. The combination was irresistible to the media as it played out like a Hollywood movie. "So yeah, this kind of thing does happen here in Orange County."

He noticed that the young crowd around him was watching them. Since neither of them was in uniform nor did they have *detective* written on their foreheads, it wasn't their jobs that caused people to watch; they just didn't quite fit in with the upscale clientele of this coffee shop. A skinny brunette with an asymmetrical haircut seemed to be writing the next *War and Peace* and kept looking up furtively as if their conversation disrupted her work. Finally, Detective Sanders nodded at her and his athletic good looks, along with his warm smile, seemed to satisfy her and she went back to her frenzy of typing.

"There's always a sexual side in these cases," said Sanders. "This is what will need to be investigated. We'll need to know all about her husband..."

"It's always the husband," said Mahoney, as he brushed off the crumbs from his jacket and wiped his mouth. "Although here in the land of the rich and richer it could also be her best friend, her boyfriend or the wife of her lover. Let's face it; It could realistically be anyone."

"True. In any event, we have our work cut out for us don't we?" Sanders picked up both coffee cups and tossed them in the trash. "Let's get back to work."

Chapter 5

Hunter King had been working on a detailed email to a former business partner when the doorbell rang. He was in his office and so focused on what he was about to write that he didn't hear the bell at first. Usually Amelia, the housekeeper, was somewhere in the house scrubbing floors or ironing sheets, but today she needed the day off for a doctor's appointment. He paused for a second, trying to decide if it was worth getting up to get the door or to ignore it. It was probably just another Amazon package sent here for Logan, his new girlfriend. That woman could order a lot of stuff. The doorbell rang again and this time more urgently, so he left the email unfinished and went to the front door of his 5-bedroom 4-bath Pelican Hill home. He opened to find two men standing there. They both looked grim.

"May I help you?" Hunter King asked, wondering if these two men were lost and needed directions. People rarely came to visit these days and when the bell rang it was always a package. No one ever seemed to need a cup of sugar as in this neighborhood no one seemed to use it much.

"Mr. King," said the younger man. "May we come in?"

"Can you first tell me who you are and why you are here?" he asked, his six-foot-two-inch former football player frame blocking the entrance. "I can't just let you in."

"Mr. King, I am Detective Martin Sanders, and this is my partner Jim, I mean James, Mahoney. We have some bad news I'm afraid." This was part of the job that Sanders dreaded and up until now, he only had to deliver bad news one other time, when a 17-year-old boy was found dead in a local park from an apparent drug overdose. Visiting the parents of this child was the hardest thing he ever had to do.

The homeowner looked confused at first, but then opened the front door to let them in. "Come on in," he said gesturing for them to enter the house. They walked into the living area, which was spotless. It was as if no one ever came in here to read a book or to share a cup of tea with friends. The yellow and white designer pillows were fluffed expertly, and the cream-colored sofa appeared to have never been used. The hardwood floors were shined to a high sheen and there was not a magazine, a book or a glass to be seen.

"May we sit down?" asked Detective Mahoney, gesturing to the cream-colored sofa.

"Let's go in here," said Hunter King, steering them away from the living area to an office down a hallway to the left. They passed by a designer kitchen which also looked unused, as if no one ever cooked or ate there. There wasn't a dish to be seen anywhere. Mahoney thought for a moment that it would be strange to live in a house that no one really lived in. Why was it that rich people never appeared to really live in their houses?

After they sat down, James Mahoney delivered the news. He gave Rebekah King's ex-husband all the details he needed to know regarding her murder. Mahoney also apologized for not coming in any sooner, but the investigation took some time. Hunter King looked shocked.

"Wow!" he said after a few seconds' delay. "I don't know what to say. I am completely in shock." As he spoke, both detectives watched to see if his expressions matched what he was saying. Was he truly shocked? Did he look upset? Was he or was he not a suspect in this case? "You know," King said, his voice sounding choked up and higher than before. "Rebekah and I were separated and have been for some time. Technically she is still my wife, but the divorce papers just need to be confirmed," he cleared his throat. "It's taking longer than expected, but that seems to be the norm." He shook his head and took a deep breath. "I can't believe it. Rebekah murdered. I would have never in a million years thought that possible."

The detectives looked at each other before speaking. They already knew that the Kings were in the process of getting a divorce and that it was just days from being finalized. What surprised them was that King hadn't yet heard of the murder since It had been several hours since it had happened, and the news stations were already broadcasting it. Or did he know?

"We are very sorry for your loss," said Detective Sanders, on cue. "We do have a few questions to ask you if that's okay. We are trying to find out who would do this to your – um – wife and why it happened at a yoga gym."

"Rebekah loved to work out. She used to be a fabulous tennis player but gave it up after she had some knee issues. As a matter of fact, I think she was scheduled for a knee replacement sometime soon." He folded his hands together and leaned forward. "I don't know if she's had it done yet. We rarely speak. Wow!," he added. "Murdered. Unbelievable."

"Out of curiosity, is this the first you have heard about the death of your ex- I mean – wife? It has been on the news and I'm surprised to learn that we're the first to tell you."

"I'm sure it was on the news by now and I did hear some sirens earlier on, but I was busy this morning with some work and I didn't turn on the television." He pulled his phone from his pocket and looked down to see a few missed calls and texts. "It looks like I have a few voicemails, so someone was trying to reach me." He replaced the cell phone in his pocket.

At that moment, an attractive brunette came racing down the stairs wearing a pair of short shorts and a tank top. She saw the two detectives seated on the plush chairs and hesitated. Pulling her long chestnut hair into a ponytail, she looked at Hunter King with shock and surprise.

"Gentlemen, this is my – um - good friend Logan. She is staying here with me for a while. Logan, these two detectives are here investigating the murder of Rebekah, my wife. My soon to be ex-wife that is. I believe it's best that you return to your room and I'll let you know when I'm finished here." She nodded, glanced over at the two men and walked slowly back up the sweeping staircase. Mahoney and Sanders both took notes. The almost ex-husband of the victim was treating his girl toy like a child. This was worth noting.

"Sorry about that," said Hunter unapologetically. "So, where was I? Ah yes. I was telling you how I hadn't had time to watch the news this morning or even pick up my phone, so yes, you were the first to give me the bad news. I'm not sure if that's really much of an honor." Mahoney looked at Sanders. They both were thinking that the woman's husband was taking the news very well. Too well.

"Is there anything else you can tell us about Rebekah that might help in the investigation?" Mahoney wanted to get as much as possible out of the man before they took off. It was still early in the investigation and they didn't need to press him too hard this early in the game.

"There really isn't a whole lot to say gentlemen. I mean, she was a difficult woman and we had our problems, but murder? I'm having a terrible time understanding how this could have ever happened. It's really just hitting me now and I don't think I'm in any state of mind to help you. Let me think this over and we can resume this conversation at a later date." The color had drained from his face making him look much older than his age. He lowered himself to the nearest armchair and put his head in his hands.

"We'll give you some time and then come back to see you," said Mahoney reluctantly. He didn't believe that Hunter King would flee the area and they had no real reason to take him in for questioning either. Not yet anyway. "Take it easy and let us know if you think of anything that could be important in this investigation."

Hunter King nodded. "Whatever I can do to help," he said getting up from his chair. He was eager to have the men leave.

As they walked back to their car, Mahoney looked over at his partner and said, "He knew about this long before we arrived, and his reaction was staged. No one is that cool after learning that his wife was brutally murdered. I don't care how lousy the marriage was."

Sanders nodded plunging his hands into his pants pockets. "I believe that bimbo girl toy he keeps upstairs also knew. What do you think?"

"I think we may have our first suspect."

Chapter 6

Jessica got on the phone and called every single employee on her contact list. Then she called the cleaning service to ask if they ever showed up after the party and if so, why was it left in such a state of disarray? She was put on hold for a few minutes while the distraught manager went to find out exactly what had happened. It was a relatively new service for the studio as their previous cleaning service had gone out of business. It was clear that the manager wanted to keep the studio as a client, so he would do whatever was necessary to keep them happy. He came back and told her that there must have been some misunderstanding; they had the date for the following week. He was terribly sorry for the mistake and offered her a 25 percent discount on their next service. Under normal circumstances, she would have been furious and given them a warning, but under the circumstances she just let it go.

Regarding the contact list, most of them had already heard from the local news agencies carrying *Breaking News* stories within hours of the event. She was glad she hadn't been interviewed by the local news stations; she had nothing really to say.

She made a cup of hot tea and took her phone off the charger and started calling. A few staff members were on vacation somewhere far away and exotic, but everyone still local had heard the news on the local TV stations or on CNN. Stories like this made for high ratings and all the media outlets jumped on it. Rich white lady found dead in yoga studio. As of now no suspects. Everyone from Bakersfield to San Diego was glued to the set because everyone loves a good drama. There was something about sunny Southern California and yoga, and when murder is added to the mix, you have a big story.

She left several voicemails and tried to keep the fatigue out of her voice. This was her chance to sink or swim and she really needed to swim. She decided to let only the Pilates instructors who had a following make the calls to both notify their clients and then to reschedule if possible. She prepped them all with an acceptable way to handle the situation.

Jessica felt exhausted. The party, the lack of sleep; It was all too much. She didn't require eight hours of sleep every night and could manage just fine on six, but the stress of all these events took a toll. After she left about a dozen messages, she took a hot shower, washed her long hair and then wrapped herself up in her coziest bathrobe. She poured herself a glass of wine to help her get through the next batch of calls.

Jessica Howard had the background to do more than just manage a yoga/Pilates studio. She had a degree in communications from the University of Southern California where she had graduated Magna Cum Laude several years earlier.

After graduation, she went to work at a boutique public relations firm, but the long hours and constant deadlines played havoc with her health. She had not only inherited her mother's super-model looks, but she had also inherited her outwardly calm demeanor and inner turmoil. The long hours and sleepless nights resulted in a drinking problem. She also got too cozy with Xanax which helped her get through the sleepless nights.

Jessica knew she didn't have to work, or she could always do odd jobs for her dad, who had his fingers in a lot of local pies, but she still wanted a challenge. When a friend told her that a new yoga studio was looking for a competent manager, she decided to give it a go. She interviewed with Spencer while Jake sat by and listened, pretending to be interested. Spencer was impressed with her beauty and serenity, which were unwritten requirements for the job. He had interviewed other competent and attractive women, but none as polished as Jessica.

She was never one of those traveling millennials who took gap years in order to visit remote places that most people had never heard of. She preferred the routine that a job required of her. Maybe it was seeing her socialite mom flit from one fund raiser and one luncheon to another that made her want to go to work every day.

Spencer and even Jake were happy with her performance. They had been managing yoga studios for some time and they were used to flighty managers so having someone as competent as Jessica, was a real blessing. The pay was slightly above average and the demands high. Studio managers were stuck dealing with teachers whose big egos caused scheduling problems and students who expected miracles from three sessions a week. It took a special person to be willing to take on this job for the so-so pay and not throw in the towel after six months. Jessica Howard was a perfect match. She was smart, competent and beautiful. They had found the ideal person for the job.

Jessica decided to start by calling the entire staff to let them know what the next few days entailed. They probably all knew anyway, but it was important to stay in touch and let them know they would be paid for the next few days. She then took the entire studio contact list, composed an informative email and sent it off. It took her well over an hour to figure out the best way to handle it. Spencer had called her earlier saying that it would be another day before they could catch a flight home. She knew it wasn't true and they had decided to stay in paradise just a few more days. That was okay; she could handle it better without them hanging over her shoulder.

As she started to call Declan Stevens, she remembered he had popped into the studio right when the investigation was beginning. Why did he need to be there? It seemed odd to her, but then again, he didn't live far away, and he was very attached to the job. He was a popular teacher and had a large following, especially among women. His athletic good looks combined with the fact he was straight – a rarity in this business – made him a big hit with the female crowd. The men liked him too because he knew how to teach movements that appealed to men. The gay men were all convinced he was closeted and just hadn't met the right guy. Declan was good at his job, too. He took the requisite workshops, had a great sense of humor and was attentive without being pushy. Jessica had hired male yoga teachers before, but some of them were too hands-on with the women. Time and time again she had to take complaints from angry women about one teacher who got just a little too touchy-feely when making an adjustment. When she finally let the guy go, other students were furious, saying he was the best teacher on staff. She often felt like she couldn't win.

Yet despite all the personnel problems and dealing with the finicky owners who were always on her about something, she had never had to deal with a murder. A woman was murdered right next to one of the reformers and handling this situation was going to be a very special kind of challenge.

Chapter 7

Detective James Mahoney came home to an empty house. His wife was working late that night and he suddenly remembered that she gave him this information earlier in the day, before he left for work, the same time she advised him that there was a hamburger thawing out in the fridge. "I'll leave you some roasted cauliflower," she said earlier that morning while cleaning a few things in the kitchen. "It's bad enough you continue to eat red meat, but I won't let you have French fries with your burger. It's time you started to watch what you eat." He pretended to act all pissed off about having to eat vegetables instead of fried potatoes, but he was pleased that she cared enough to make healthy meals.

James and his wife Lizzie lived in Orange, a town north and east of Newport Beach, so he had a relatively short commute to the office. Lizzie was a neo-natal nurse at a nearby hospital. They had been married for 32 years and their one and only daughter Michelle lived in Minneapolis; they rarely spoke. It was hard, of course, since she was their only daughter, but over time they got used to the fact that she had chosen to distance herself from her family. It became harder after she married and had twin boys, who were now a bit over two years old. They were notified of the birth and received a host of baby pictures of their chubby dark-haired grandsons. Every Christmas James and Lizzie received a card with the four of them standing around a scene straight out of a Christmas fairytale. The note on the card was the same as it was for everyone else on their list. *"Merry Christmas to all."* Lizzie handled the situation better than he ever could; she handled most situations better than he ever could. Her take on it was that she did everything she could to raise her only daughter, including providing a loving home, a college education and a place to stay after graduation. "I did what I could and if that wasn't enough, I just don't know what to say," Lizzie admitted over a second glass of wine one night. "We bring these children into the world and the rest is up to them."

Mahoney attributed his wife's cavalier attitude to her profession. She had seen a lot over the years, and it made her tough. He saw a lot too, but in his case, it was domestic violence, accidental drug overdoses and people who simply disappeared. His years on the police force had shown him the seedier side of life, even here in wealthy Orange County. It wasn't all that different now that he was a detective, he just had to dig deeper into what made people act in a certain way.

He took out the thin hamburger patty and heated it on the grill. He arranged a salad of lettuce, pickles and a few slices of organic tomatoes which Lizzie insisted on getting from the local farmer's market. He found the roasted cauliflower in a bright red container in the fridge. He pulled it out and opened the lid, smelled it and decided to eat it the next day. He then searched around in the kitchen cabinet for a bag of Cheetos or chips but just found some organic chips that he was convinced were dry and tasteless. If he was going to eat junk, he wanted the real deal. He poured himself a glass of lime-flavored sparkling water and tossed in a couple of ice cubes. There were a few cans of beer in the fridge, but he knew better than to touch them. They were for Lizzie. After a few years of putting up with his hard drinking, Liz gave him the ultimatum. "It's me or the booze, my love," she stated. "You start AA, or I start cleaning out your closet." Now five years and a few months later, he could honestly say that the 12-step program worked. He didn't go to meetings like he used to, but he followed the steps religiously. He didn't even mind when his wife poured herself the occasional drink while he sipped on fizzy water.

With Lizzie gone, he set his place in front of the TV. For some reason, that drove his wife crazy. She felt that dinner should be eaten at the table and that conversation should be civil. It had always been that way when Michelle was a child. Now it almost seemed pointless as they didn't have nearly as much to talk about. He could have discussed his cases, but he preferred leaving all that at the office; none of it made for good dinner conversation. She felt the same way about things she saw every day, although every once in a while, she shared a lovely success story from the ward.

He turned on the local news station to see what they were reporting. A skinny blonde with very large breasts was giving a weather report. Weather here in Southern California was rarely interesting or newsworthy as it was pretty much always the same. No wonder they hired women who looked like Playboy models. She moved around showing her long-tanned legs and then reported that there would be another week of 72 degrees and sunny skies with a very slight chance of rain on Wednesday.

The anchor was back on air saying that right after the commercial break they would report on a murder at a local yoga studio. The detective sighed and took a large bite out of his burger. People in this area loved this kind of news. It was very Hollywood and would probably eventually be used as the basis for a screenplay. He used to feel a twinge of excitement being involved in these kinds of investigations, but that was no longer the case. He just wanted to get to the bottom of it and figure out who killed Rebekah King.

Chapter 8

Jessica finally finished calling everyone she needed to contact. She had planted herself at the kitchen table with a pot of boiling water, some organic tea and her phone. She was even able to trace the two yoga teachers who were off at a retreat somewhere trying to tune out the world. She felt terrible bursting their meditative bubble, but she felt they needed to hear it first from her before reading it somewhere or picking it up as local gossip. Even at retreats, gossip travels. After all the exclamations and shocked replies, everyone wanted to know when they would be able to return to work. Her answer was she would let them know as soon as possible. What she didn't tell them was that earning the reputation as a local yoga/Pilates studio where a client was murdered was not going to bode well for their business. Spencer and Jake were already looking into crisis control companies that could help them put a positive spin on it. After failing to find a good alternative to their return flight, they decided to stay put. Jessica could handle it. She just needed some professional help to turn it around. In the meantime, it was up to her to encourage the staff to talk to clients and students as much as possible and restore a sense of peace. Many of the yoga and Pilates teachers socialized to a certain extent with their students and had their contact information. Of course, the local competition was going to have a heyday with this, although their first reaction was to call or email their sympathies to her. That won't last, Jessica thought as she read through the emails and texts. The competition for clientele was fierce in this community. There were several studios and gyms that offered similar services and although Newport Yoga and Pilates prided itself on only hiring the most qualified instructors, most people didn't care or notice. All they wanted was someone who looked good and gave them the feeling that this stuff really worked. Within five blocks there were three private Pilates studios, two gyms and a new mind/body center opening up just two blocks down the road. There was a lot of money here and a lot of people, but even with the dense population, there was just too much choice available. She knew it was just a matter of time before the competition took all this information about the murder and ran with it. She could even see the Instagram posts "No one gets murdered here."

She went through her list of names again and saved Becca Chen for last. She really liked Becca because she was a little older and had many years of teaching experience under her belt. She also got along well with almost everyone and had an easy-going temperament that Jess found refreshing. Yoga and Pilates people, despite their reputation for being calm and spiritual, tended to be a neurotic bunch. The yoga people wanted everyone to believe that they were not materialistic yet showed up to class in late model luxury cars and expensive yoga gear. The Pilates instructors, although cut from a different cloth, tended to be fiercely competitive with one another. Becca had been an investment banker in another life and after retiring a millionaire at age 37, she started teaching her one real love, yoga. She was still very attractive at the age of 48.

"Becca," said Jessica when she reached her on the phone. Jessica was relaxed, dressed in an old pair of cheap yoga pants and some old-fashioned pink leg warmers she had found years ago at a vintage clothing store. She had a cup of steaming hot tea in her hands and her dog, Harry, was at her side. The windows were open, and the room smelled of freshly cut grass. A flock of birds sang a melody in the background.

"Jess. I heard the news. This is terrible. Just terrible. I can't even imagine what you are going through. Were you the one that found the body?"

"Not me. No. Monica was the first to find her. She opened up that morning and found her lying next to the reformer. Poor girl called me right away. Anyway, I called to ask you a few questions." Jessica eased her body onto her bed waiting for a response. She needed to ask these questions so she could learn something about the victim. She knew it wasn't her job to investigate, but she wanted to know more.

"Oh! That's terrible. Poor Monica. I don't know what I would have done if it had been me."

"None of us can imagine how terrible it must have been. Monica may never get over this."

"No. I hope she seeks out some sort of therapy. Poor girl."

Jessica sighed remembering just how traumatized Monica was. Harry snuggled up onto her lap and began licking her arm. She pulled him closer as she continued talking. "Anyway, the reason I am calling you is to ask a few questions if you don't mind."

"Not at all. What can I do for you?" Someone was calling for Becca in the background and it sounded as if it could be one of her children. Jessica tried to remember if Becca ever discussed her children with her, but she couldn't remember much about them.

"I was hoping you might be able to shed some light on Rebekah. Any small detail that might be of some help. I know she often went to your Tuesday morning flow class and she seemed to be a big fan of yours." Teachers were always flattered when someone became both a fan and a follower.

"Yes. I think she was a regular in that class. Good student, too. Moved well for her age. Although there are many women in their 40s and 50s who move well," she added. "I noticed her. I thought she may have had a dance or athletic background. Pretty lady. Not that it matters."

Jessica remembered checking in Rebekah a few times and taking notice of her lovely complexion. She didn't look to be 30 as so many middle-aged women tried to do, but she had a natural glow that was unusual for her age. Even with all the med spas and first-rate plastic surgeons in the area, not everyone looked as young as they wanted to. There was something more to Rebekah King than flawless skin. She just *seemed* younger.

"You know," said Becca, "I rarely socialize with my students. I know that other teachers do, and they end up with quite a following, but it never seemed right to me." She cleared her throat and continued. "It's a personal choice, and for me teaching yoga is both a hobby and a job, but not a way to socialize. I have friends from other aspects of my life, and I don't need to be buddies with my students or clients." Jessica agreed with this, but at the same time she knew that many teachers frequently hung out with their students. There was no policy against it, although it did get troublesome at times. The problem they had with a student/teacher relationship was that if the teacher left the studio, the student might follow. Or, if a romance developed and there was trouble, the student would not only leave but also would make negative comments on social media, making it a disaster control situation. This was why it was so crucial to hire only the best teachers available. If they decided to date or even become friends with the clientele there wasn't much one could do.

"Jess, I'm truly sorry this happened. I know it will be a strain on the studio for a while, but things will get back to normal soon enough. People seem to have short memories these days. Something may seem dreadful one day and then out of the news cycle the next." Becca's words were a big comfort to the manager. She had a way of doing that. The perfect yoga teacher.

"Thank you. I do appreciate the help. If you think of something – anything at all - please let me know. Even the smallest details can help." "You know, there is something now that I think of it," Becca said thoughtfully. Jessica sat up quickly. This was the first time someone had said something that sounded promising. She had asked other teachers, and no one seemed to know much of anything. Becca continued, "A few weeks ago, I think it was, I was over at Kean's Coffee getting something to go when I noticed Rebekah sitting toward the back of the store. At first, I wasn't sure it was her, but she has that cute pink jacket that she sometimes wears to class, and I remember once telling her how much I liked it. Anyway, she wasn't alone so I glanced over to see who she might be sharing a coffee with and it was Declan. I was surprised. I didn't know they knew each other as his style of teaching is very different from mine. I didn't want to stare, but I have to say they looked quite cozy. I left the store and quickly forgot about it. I had other things on my mind. And let's face it, it isn't all that unusual to see our students socialize with our teachers. But since you asked, I thought I would relay that to you." She took in a deep breath. "I would never have told anyone that because it sounds so gossipy, but given the circumstances, I thought it best that I let you know." Becca sounded relieved to have told Jess.

"Of course, Becca. Thank you. That's helpful and the kind of information I need to give to the detectives." She wrote it down so she could let them know as soon as possible. Declan Stevens. What was Rebekah King doing cozying up him at a coffee shop anyway?

Chapter 9

After calling the principal detective assigned to the case, Jessica decided to look into Declan Stevens' background. She had seen his resume before, but now it was time to take a second look. She dug through all the staff bios until she found it. When Spencer and Jake had taken over the small all-purpose gym three years ago and added it to their LA empire of trendy and chic yoga/Pilates studios, Declan was one of the first to be hired. of course, the two owners would be drawn to the good-looking 33-year-old with the body of a Greek god. She could actually visualize Spencer feeling a twinge of envy after seeing the new teacher's sexy young body. Spencer was the older of the two, and he was deeply aware of the age difference between Jake and himself. They were just seven years apart, but sometimes Jake made it feel like decades. Jake was also in better shape and better looking, and he flaunted it. He often joked how he married Spencer for his brains and not his looks. That would upset Spencer, but he kept his thoughts to himself. Poor Spencer had to deal with it day in and day out, but they loved each other, and they made it work, no different than a lot of men and women she knew who had balance issues in their marriage.

Declan, at the time, was an actor wannabe living in Long Beach, trying to make some extra money as a yoga teacher. His training had been good enough for the studio at the time. The owners were looking more for attractive younger teachers who knew how to move and could bring in the crowds. Declan could bring in the older women who longed for an escape from their dull marriages and privileged lives. Gay men loved his class and even straight men appreciated his strength and ability to do some crazy poses. His training was adequate; he had studied with a local LA yoga rock star who had put together a decent training program in Santa Monica. Later on, this celebrity Svengali ended up in court with a series of harassment charges against him, but despite all that, his reputation as a yoga master prevailed.

Jessica pulled out her laptop and Googled Declan Stevens. She found his information on their own yoga site, an article that was now more than two years old, naming him as one of the sexiest bachelors in Orange County and then making a reference to a small role he had in a B movie with limited release. There were also many pictures from his Instagram feed. She tried several other search engines to see if she could get some more detailed information. She followed a link on one of these search engines to see if there was more. She tried a few more links and discovered a small obituary from Omaha, Nebraska. It mentioned that the deceased left behind two sons and a daughter. The son was born David Petrie and was now known as Declan Stevens. So, thought Jessica as she perused the article, he had changed his name professionally. It wasn't unusual for people in the entertainment profession to change their names from the ordinary to the more exotic, it happened all the time. Yet Jessica was surprised that she didn't know this before. Usually there was a question somewhere in the job application paperwork asking if they had ever been known by another name. Was he hiding something or was it just his humble Nebraska roots? She then searched the father's name. She got very little information other than what was mentioned in the original obituary. His name was also David Petrie and before he passed away back in 2016, he was a clerk at a DMV just outside the city of Omaha. His wife Alice was deceased, leaving behind the three children.

She tucked that bit of information away, thinking it might come in handy later on. She decided that she would let the detectives figure this out on their own as that was their job. She was willing to put in some of the work in addition to her real job – the one that paid her.

She opened the fridge to see if there was an open bottle of wine, and when she didn't find one she shut the door. It wasn't time to open a new bottle, but she really felt the need for a cold glass of wine. There was still a lot to do and she needed to keep her wits about her. The rest of the employees needed to be contacted and she had to get the studio open once and for all. One more day of keeping it closed to tie up loose ends and then the doors had to be re-opened. The clientele would only wait so long before heading down the road half a mile to another studio that was probably feeding off of her studio's crisis by offering two-for-one classes. Jessica was on a serious time crunch.

She tried to remember Declan that night at the party. How was he acting? Did he seem in good spirits? Was he even with the victim during the course of the event? She was so busy making sure that glasses were filled that she hardly noticed anyone. When she wasn't clearing off empty wine glasses or restocking the veggie tray, she was observing the crowd to make sure everyone had what they needed. Small groups of students and teachers were forming based who took whose class and everyone seemed to be having a great time. She knew Declan was there, but everything else was a blank. The entire evening was a blur to her.

She thought it through. In all the time she knew Declan, she never had any real problem with him. He had a big ego, but who didn't these days? With his looks and sex appeal, an oversized ego was to be expected. He was no different from any of the other good-looking 30-somethings who had their eyes on Hollywood. No, she thought as she snapped her laptop shut. Despite the date at Kean's Coffee that Becca reported to her, she didn't believe that Declan Stevens was capable of murder.

Chapter 10

Hunter King liked order in his life. He liked to get up at 7 a.m., a bit later on the weekends, have his strong coffee and buttered toast followed by a three-mile run. On the days that he didn't run, he went to the gym to meet with his personal trainer for an hour. Then he would return home, have a light snack and go upstairs to check on Logan. She could sleep all day if he let her. He liked to get into bed next to her nudging her just enough so she would wake up.

After Logan woke up and did her morning exercise routine, they would go out and do something fun. She liked to go shopping at Southcoast Plaza to see all the latest fashions in fitness and casual wear. Some days she hovered around the chic jewelry stores to see what kind of mood her sugar daddy was in. They would wander into one of the over-priced and trendy restaurants for a bite of lunch. Hunter felt proud walking around the beautiful shopping mall with his stunning girlfriend. They got a lot of looks from both men and women; the men were envious of his good fortune and the women were jealous of Logan's perfect face and body. No question about it, she was hot. When she wore those extra short denim shorts, he could barely control himself. She was no rocket scientist, that was for sure, but at this stage of his life he didn't want someone to challenge him; a willing partner with a hot willing body was all he needed. When this got old, there would be lots of other younger and sexier women who would be eager to jump into his bed. He still looked good for a 55-year-old and if that didn't attract them, his ample wealth certainly would.

He had fallen out of love with Rebekah a long time ago. She had become so difficult and unattractive to him. They had only been married a few years before her very presence made him feel ill. How many times had he wished she would jump off a cliff or drop dead in one of those exercise classes she was always taking? He often wondered what he saw in her in the first place. She was attractive, but no beauty. Her nose was a bit too wide, but she refused to have it fixed even though he suggested it time and time again. His best buddy Joe Shapiro was the best plastic surgeon in town, but she refused to do anything about it. Now he realized she did it to spite him. If he had told her he loved her nose she would have made an appointment the next day.

That was Rebekah. Always doing things to spite him but in such a way that only he noticed. Textbook passive aggressive. Everyone else thought she was an angel.

He tapped Logan on the shoulder to wake her up; it was past 10 a.m. and the morning was getting away from them. He had no idea how she could sleep so late. She was in a deep sleep and the $375 light blue teddy with the white embroidered flowers was pushed up high showing the matching bikini panties. His felt his heart racing, along with an intense stirring in his pants and he wanted nothing more than to shake her awake and seduce her, but it was too late, and they needed to get going. As sexy and willing as she was, he had too much on his mind now to carry through. It would be just a matter of time before the detectives were back prying into his life and trying to peg him as the number one suspect. It was always the husband, or so they believed. He would have to convince them otherwise, but it wouldn't be easy.

Logan was sound asleep and he enjoyed watching her. She was so young and fresh and his desire for her was growing by the second. He put his large hand on her back and gave her a gentle shake. She began to stir. He called her name, and she opened her eyes and rolled onto her back. "Want to join me?" she said in a sleepy voice as she reached for him with her slender arms. "The bed is nice and warm." Hunter King couldn't resist her. He quickly undressed and jumped into bed with her. The shopping could wait. Now that Rebekah was gone, life was going to get a lot easier for him.

Chapter 11

Detective Mahoney went through his notes and tried to put two and two together, but he came up with nothing. Everyone was being cooperative, but other than the ex-husband, there were no real suspects. Rebekah King appeared to have no real enemies other than her ex-husband or almost ex-husband and he wasn't even sure that was the case. Not yet anyway. Amazing, he thought. She was well-liked in the community and at the yoga studio where she spent several hours stretching, chanting and doing whatever it was they did at these places. Everyone seemed both shocked and saddened by her death and as of this moment, no one seemed to have much of a motive.

There was a tap on his office door, and he shouted to his caller to come in. The detective liked working with the door closed even when he wasn't doing anything important or urgent. Even at home, he liked his door closed; it seemed to keep the outside world outside of his inner orbit. His partner Sanders walked in, his head hanging low. He looked like he hadn't slept for days. His thick hair was uncombed and stood in spikes on top of his head and he had large dark circles under his eyes. His clothes were rumpled, and Mahoney could smell a vague unwashed odor coming off his partner's body.

"The wife kick you out last night?" asked the older detective without taking his eyes off his notes. This was the second time this week that Detective Sanders looked like he could use a change of clothes and a good hot shower. "I could smell you walk in."

"No," was the only answer Sanders gave as he sat down and began to review his own list of notes. Detective Mahoney let it go. He would have to bring it up sooner or later, but now there were more important things to do, like figuring out how to go about this investigation. He realized that sooner rather than later he would have to have a talk with his partner on moderately good grooming.

"The cause of death was strangulation." said Sanders as he reviewed what was in front of him. "There was no sign of rape and other than a few scratches on her arms, no sign of a struggle. In other words, she probably knew the killer."

Mahoney looked up. He tried to look past the messy hair and the face that desperately needed a shave. Good thing the young man was attractive because that, at this time, was his only saving grace. "Are you telling me or asking me?"

"Neither, boss. Just stating a fact, I guess"

"You guess? Well, you guessed correctly. It seems that there was very little struggle if any. Forensics shows that she may have had sexual intercourse shortly before her death as it looks like there was some penetration, but as you said there was no semen, so whoever it was never finished the job." He looked up to see his partner still looking down. He continued on. "She appeared to have died quickly so whoever did this to her was strong enough to take care of it quickly. My first guess is it was a man."

"So what now? Do we go after the husband or see what else we can dig up?"

The senior detective stood up and put both of his hands in his pants pockets. He then walked over to the small window and looked out at the clear blue sky that was typical this time of year.

"We need to talk to her close friends. Apparently, she wasn't one to travel in packs and do the lunch thing at Fashion Island, but she must have had some friends. Don't most women have friends?" He walked back to his desk. "I know my Lizzie does. She needs her one night out a week with the ladies to drink and complain about the men in their lives."

His partner shrugged. He ran his hand through his thick, messy hair and looked down at his crumpled appearance as if noticing it for the first time.

"I wouldn't know much about that these days. Katie left me about three months ago. Even when we were together, she kept a lot of her personal life separate from me. I was gone so much anyway, working cases, that I hardly noticed if she went out or not." He sniffed his armpits and made a face. "Geez boss, you should have told me I stunk like frat house on a Sunday morning. I had no idea I was this bad."

"You may want to check out your sense of smell," replied Mahoney. "They say that's the first thing to go."

"I'll take some time to shower and get a change of clothes if you don't mind. I don't think I can show up talking to the elite women of Newport Beach smelling like stale beer. I don't think they'd want to stick around very long."

"Nope, that's for sure. Why don't you take an hour and I'll start going through some names. I can get a start with that creep of a husband, as I'm sure he is aware of at least one good friend. From there, if the women talk, I can get exactly what I need." Sanders grabbed his things and started for the door. It was still early enough that he could afford the time to go home and clean up.

"Oh, and Sanders. Don't forget to use deodorant. It works wonders."

"Right boss. I'll try to remember. Thanks for the great advice." They both laughed.

Mahoney picked up the phone and dialed Hunter King's cell phone. At least he could leave a message. If King was guilty of killing his wife, he'd be ready and willing to give out the names of her former friends. Shift the blame to someone else. Mahoney knew from several years of experience that everybody had an enemy somewhere, and Rebekah King would be no exception.

Chapter 12

1999 – Boston, Massachusetts

Everyone was getting ready for Y2K, the year 2000, the end of a millennium. The beginning of a new century. Some expected the end of civilization while others were hoping for a historic year-end blockbuster party. Rebekah King was still relatively new in the city and was just getting used to her job and her new digs. One of the top real estate companies in Boston had hired her as an office manager while she studied for her real estate license. It was a good deal and the pay was decent. She had her small apartment a mile and a half from the office and she could walk or take the train which the locals called The T just about anywhere. She sold her 1995 Camry shortly after she arrived in Boston from Los Angeles. In Southern California, a car was a necessity, but here it wasn't. She figured if she ever wanted to get outside the city for a day or two, she could always rent a car. She kept her California driver's license instead of waiting in line at the DMV to get a Massachusetts one. If she ended up staying long enough, she would consider a car, but not now.

She loved Boston. She loved the history, the great seafood and the funny Bostonian accent that made her giggle. Granted, she had yet to spend a winter here battling the cold, wind and snow. As she was a Southern California girl, the long cold winters could come as a shock, but for the time being she was loving everything about the city. She arrived in April, so she only experienced the rainy spring, the warm summer and now, the glorious fall season. She had always heard about the beautiful New England autumns and now she was lucky enough to experience one for herself.

She left Los Angeles in such a hurry that she didn't pack everything she needed. She brought two full suitcases and one small duffel bag which was mostly filled with clothes, books, cosmetics and a few odds and ends. She thought about all the things left behind in her 3500 sq. foot Pacific Palisades home, like the exquisite watercolor that she received as a birthday gift from her husband two years ago. He bought it from a young up-and-coming local artist whose work often sold in the six-figure range. The lovely painting hung over the mantel, its aqua blue and greens a glorious complement to the soft leather sofa that cost a small fortune. At the time, she appreciated the house for its ample size and splendid décor. Usually that type of ostentation didn't mean much to her but waking up in her king-sized bed in her large master bedroom became a nice way to start the day.

She left a closet full of designer clothes including Gucci, Prada, Michael Kors and Chanel. Her 125-plus pairs of shoes lined the shelves of the walk-in closet. She would have been happy with an ordinary closet and a shoe rack, but in these larger homes a big walk-in closet was de rigueur. She was able to squeeze three pairs of shoes into one of her suitcases and left the rest behind. She could always get a few pairs of Skechers if she needed to. She would need a good pair of winter boots so she could trudge through the heavy snow which actually sounded like fun.

Finding herself in a new city, a city so different than Los Angeles, she felt reborn. She could be anyone she wanted to be and leave her old self behind. Back on the West Coast, she kept to herself only making friends with people that traveled in her inner circles. She wasn't one to chit-chat with other women unless it was absolutely necessary. Money was never an issue for her so even the prospect of having to watch her budget a bit sounded like a fun challenge. She would be like a starving artist or college student that had to make choices like food or underwear. She could easily afford both with the money she had put away in a separate account, but it was fun to pretend.

Now that she was here in Boston, Rebekah chose a small but cozy apartment right in the heart of the city. She knew eventually she would outgrow it, but for now it was fun being able to walk out the door and find an ethnic restaurant within a short walk. She had only been to the East Coast a few times but never to Boston. She loved the big city feel in a relatively smaller city. It was very manageable and not all spread out like Los Angeles.

She didn't miss her friends from California at all. *Friends* was a term she used loosely; they were never real friends like the ones she made when she was a young girl. When she felt obligated to organize events or parties, she invited people who fit into her LA lifestyle. Minor celebrities, screen writers, high-powered attorneys and business owners all clinked champagne flutes together in celebration of one victory or another.

She never enjoyed those parties but put on a brave and happy face. She played the part well and no one, not even those screenwriters with their degrees from fancy East Coast schools, could sense she was putting on an act. She was pretty enough, funny and a marvelous hostess.

Then one day it became just too much. She was tired of the perpetual Southern California sunshine and the façade of great new wealth. She would be happy if she never again saw a Ferrari racing down the 405. She just needed to get away as soon as possible.

As she threw a few things into the expensive suitcase that was a Christmas gift, Rebekah realized that there was nothing at all she liked about her current life. Everything was too easy and spoon fed. She remembered leaving her own family not that many years ago for similar reasons, although they didn't have the wealth and glamour of the life she had now. None of it was what she wanted.

She grabbed a piece of paper, wrote a note to her husband and then called a cab to take her to Los Angeles International Airport, known to all Californians as LAX.

Chapter 13

"That detective called me and wanted a list of Rebekah's closest friends," Hunter scratched his head as his girlfriend lay on the sofa in a white lacy sports bra and a pair of tight blue yoga pants. She was watching some annoying reality show and drinking a protein shake that looked like Pepto Bismol. She was just so damn hot, but her lack of brains was starting to irritate him. Why couldn't she have both? In any event, having those detectives sniff around the premises did little or nothing for his desire.

"Well, we were together that entire night, weren't we?" she piped in while turning the pages of a fashion magazine during a television commercial. He had an entire library of great books and she never so much as looked at them. Instead she subscribed to magazines that gave advice on how to get rid of frizzy hair prior to giving the world's best blow job. He was okay with that, but there were times when he wished they had something to talk about other than the latest handbag from Louis Vuitton. "I think that was the night we had dinner over at Richie's apartment and then came back here and fucked on the floor," she said nonchalantly. "I remember that night vividly. How could I forget?" She looked up at him innocently. Her voice got childlike which used to turn him on, but now it just made him feel stupid. At least with Rebekah, she was intelligent enough to hold his interest even when their sex life turned dull.

Most of the time, Logan's overt sexuality and total lack of inhibitions would drive him mad with desire, but now, given current circumstances, it was becoming annoying. She didn't comprehend the severity of a murder investigation. Did she even understand that he was potentially the chief suspect? She would make a terrible witness, but he knew she had to be an alibi at some point or another. She was too dumb to be credible anyway. He was no fool; she was in this for the money and the prestige.

Logan Watson came from a lower middle-class family near Bakersfield. She was blessed with super-model good looks and enough sense to know that her looks were her key to success. Her beauty was what got her out of Bakersfield and into a Newport Beach mansion. If she had been a plain Jane, she would still be working at a fast-food restaurant serving people from a drive-thru window. She would be able to play the looks card for another five to ten years, but then it would start to wear thin. There was always someone younger, prettier and sexier and she would have to find a way to make her own living.

Yet right now she was all Hunter had. She was happy and comfortable with the relationship and didn't seem eager to move on to someone else. He provided the expensive clothes and accessories while she provided the arm candy he needed to show everyone just how well he was doing. The sex was good, too. He was confident that she would stick by him for as long as he continued to shower money on her. They were currently planning a trip to France and Italy for later in the year and another one at a five-star resort in Aspen. She loved the closet full of high-end fashion and she spent hours each week organizing her shoes. For the time being, it was a win-win situation. Now she had to use whatever smarts the good Lord gave her to help him clear his name. He was well aware of the fact that he would be a primary suspect and he needed all the help he could get.

Chapter 14

At one time, Angela Demarco was Rebekah King's best friend. They had been good friends since joining a local women's group that got together once a month. The purpose of the group was to discuss everything from gardening, to the latest fashions, to low calorie cooking. It was a group set out with all the best intentions, but in time turned into a wine and whine group of upper middle-class ladies in unhappy marriages. Detective Mahoney learned about Angela from Jessica. She had dug up some information from a teacher who had, for a short time, befriended the victim, and she knew of Ms. Demarco.

Angela, who preferred to be called Angie, was originally from New York City. She had moved to Southern California 15 years earlier to marry an attorney she met at a mid-town Manhattan bar. He was going through a nasty divorce and she had lost her husband a year earlier in a car accident. They hit it off right away and a year later, Angie left her job as a high school Spanish teacher to move to Newport Beach where she and Tom married.

Rebekah had liked Angie because she was different from the other women in the group. She seemed more worldly, better read, and more interested in things other than lip enhancements and Botox injections. Both women took extraordinary care to keep the wrinkles away, but there was more to their lives than how young they looked. Also, Angie seemed to have a very stable and happy marriage, which was rare in this group. There were problems of course, as there are in every marriage, but she was content with what she had. Rebekah admired that quality in her.

Mahoney and Sanders rang the doorbell of Ms. Demarcos' Corona Del Mar house. The house was quite a bit smaller than Hunter King's palatial home, but it was just as elegant. The homes on this narrow, tree-lined street were smaller than some of the beach front properties, but still sold for well over $2 million. The lots were small, but the unique architecture made each and every house look like it belonged in a home and garden magazine. The Demarco's landscaping featured one of these picture-perfect lawns with a splash of color among the leafy succulents. The dark wooden front door was polished to a shine. After ringing the bell, they expected a long wait before anyone would open the door for them; no one was ever eager to let them in.

Angie, however, opened the door right away. She was dressed in a pair of cream-colored linen pants and a bright pink knit top. Her thick dark hair fell to her shoulders. She looked to be about 45, but their investigation uncovered that she was 51. With olive skin and large green eyes, she was still very attractive.

"Come on in," she said holding the door open wide. "Excuse the mess, but I am going through a few cabinets and getting rid of things. You know how it is," she said leading them through a living area that was a stark contrast to other homes they had visited on various other investigations. Unlike some other homes of the wealthy, this home looked lived in: A few books stacked on the coffee table, a pair of shoes left near the door and even a lightweight jacket draped over the sofa all gave the impression that people really lived here. "It never seems to fail that no matter how much I get rid of, I bring in even more. It's funny because I don't even really enjoy shopping, but I never seem to make a dent in any of this." She gestured to all the stuff that was lying around. "Sometimes," she added. "You just want to get rid of everything." She then opened the door to what appeared to be an office area and she invited them in. This room was neat and organized, but still gave the impression that someone worked there and it wasn't just for show. "This, gentlemen, is my office. I do my writing, my reading and anything else that is required of me these days. Come on in and take a seat." She pulled out two chairs for the detectives. "Would you like tea? Coffee? I have a pot on now. I also made some 'healthy' oatmeal cookies with organic flour, sugar and oatmeal so I have no idea how good they will taste." She emphasized the word healthy. The men agreed to a cup of coffee and some cookies. She left the room for a brief time and then returned holding a tray with three mugs of coffee and a plate of freshly baked cookies.

"I understand," said Mahoney as he grabbed two cookies off the plate. "that you and Ms. King were close friends."

"Cream? Sugar?" She asked while taking the mug off the tray.

"No. Believe it or not I take my coffee black. So," he added as he took a large bite of the cookie, "you two apparently were friends."

"We *were* friends once upon a time, but things had cooled off between us." She raised a single brow. "As a matter of fact, when I heard the news last night on the local news channel that was the first I had heard anything about Rebekah in quite some time." She broke a smaller cookie in half and then placed it down next to her coffee mug. "You could say that at one time, and not all that long ago, we were almost inseparable." She laughed. "We were almost like what today they call BFFs. Of course, we were both a little too old to be acting like teenagers, but we did spend a lot of time together and I believe we spoke on the phone almost daily."

"What did you talk about?" asked Sanders as he leaned back in the chair. Mahoney gave him a look. The woman either didn't notice or didn't care.

"Hmmm, what do middle-aged women talk about on the phone every day? Let me think about that. Well, to be truthful, a lot of our conversations were based on gossip. You have to understand that when you travel in certain circles and have a lot of time on your hands, the conversation tends to move in that direction. It's strange, but when we first met, we talked about how much we *hated* women who gossip on the phone, but we ended up doing just that. Then again..." She stopped mid-sentence and grabbed another cookie from the tray. She placed a single hand on her neck and massaged the back of it. "My poor neck," she said. "I guess I slept funny last night."

"Then again what?" asked Sanders. "You were about to say something." Mahoney sat back and let his partner take the reins. This was how the younger guys learned. Mahoney, too, had to step up when his older partner, who was now long retired, forced him to get his feet wet. He would have phrased it differently, but Sanders managed to get the point across.

"Well then again there was nothing very consistent about her. She was hot and cold, friendly and withdrawn. A study of contrasts I might say." She paused for a second and then continued. "I have to say that Rebekah started to get a bit strange all of a sudden. It began when she started having marital problems. Let's face it," Angie said, leaning back in the chair and crossing her legs. "We *all* have marital problems, but she had – how can I say this? – different problems from the rest of us." Both detectives listened intently to her. This could be a goldmine of information, but they had to play their cards right and keep her talking.

"Different?" asked Sanders. "Different in what way?"

"Hunter started having affairs a few years ago. I mean, let's get real here. Men will be men. You know that most of the men who travel in our circles are extremely successful, wealthy and are incurably Type A. This is a tried-and-true formula for cheating." She said as she re-filled her mug with hot coffee. "And let's also not forget that Orange County is teeming with beautiful young women anxious to get their hands on wealthy older men. Some of these result in broken marriages, while other women tolerate it so they can maintain their expensive lifestyles. Anyway, when Rebekah first found out about Hunter she was quite upset. We had often talked about what we would do if this happened to us and she always seemed confident she could get through it. Despite her intellect and apparent disinterest in material things, she seemed to like the lifestyle." She tilted her head to one side. "She complained about it a lot, but I think deep down she liked having all the accoutrements that come with wealth."

"This is all very interesting Ms. Demarco and we appreciate you sharing this information with us." Sanders was using a tactic that Mahoney had taught him early on: Be appreciative of the person providing information whether it was good or not. In this case it was all good. "Can you give us any background information on Mr. King?" Sanders was aware that they had already been looking into his background and his apparent wealth, but maybe she had some additional information to provide.

The investigation revealed that Hunter King came from a wealthy family of business owners. His grandfather had started a small chain of grocery stores in the Southwest and his father had continued with the legacy. Hunter received an MBA from The University of Pennsylvania and tried to branch away from the family business by starting a career in finance. He did well enough, but the real money came from a substantial inheritance when his dad passed away. As an only child he got it all. He was married once before, and that marriage produced one son. He married Rebekah just a few months after the signature on her divorce papers was dry. There were no children from this union.

They knew about the work Rebekah did before marrying her wealthy husband and how she dabbled in a few things after the wedding. She ran a small women's boutique in Laguna Beach, was a hostess at a high-end club, and eventually tried to get her real estate license which she never completed. When she got bored, she worked or took classes and when she was busy, she stopped. She enjoyed her workouts and prior to doing yoga and Pilates, she was an avid tennis player and runner. She ran three marathons in her life and many half marathons. A knee injury put a stop to the running and that was when she took up Pilates.

"Hunter was a bit of a jerk," Angie said, wrinkling her nose. "Like I said, the men in our circle tend to have huge egos, but hands down he had the biggest ego of all. At least the other men had personalities and were fun to be with. Not Hunter. He was completely lacking a sense of humor and a heart. I couldn't stand him. Never understood why she married him." She stood up and grabbed the empty coffee pot. "Would either of you care for more coffee or another cookie? Otherwise I'm going to just save these for my husband. He loves it when I bake." Both men shook their heads. Mahoney was considering taking one for the road but realized three was probably one too many.

"I have to be honest and say that I didn't really know him all that well, but what I knew wasn't good. When Rebekah and I first met, we tried doing the couples thing. You know what I mean. We did a few dinners together and we had them over for a BBQ one 4th of July but it never worked out."

"Why was that?" asked Sanders. He was furiously taking notes on his pad.

"The husbands didn't get along. Tom thought Hunter was a pompous ass and I must say, Tom was right about that. I wouldn't say my husband is the best judge of people, but he figured that one out pretty quickly."

"Can you offer any examples for us?" asked Sanders. Mahoney narrowed his eyes, but the younger detective ignored him.

"Sure," replied Angela. She sat back down and put the tray back on the table. "Once we met them at this restaurant down in Laguna Beach. It was one of those hip trendy places that lasts for a year or two and then goes out of business. Anyway, Rebekah and I thought it would be fun for the four of us to get together, walk around the town and then have a few drinks and dinner. She loved these trendy places where all the young people go to be seen. We met at our place and we decided to take our car. We had just bought a new SUV and wanted to take it for a spin. Well…"

"What kind of SUV?" asked Sanders. Again, Mahoney gave him a funny look, but said nothing.

"What kind? It was a Porsche. We still have it in the garage. Why is that relevant?"

"It isn't," replied Mahony glancing over at his partner. "Please go on."

"No sooner did we get into the car, Hunter stopped talking. He wouldn't answer any questions and he just stared out the window like a petulant two-year-old. Rebekah had no idea what was going on. Then when we arrived at the restaurant and were seated, Hunter pulled out his phone, called someone and left the table. He came back, said it was an emergency and left us."

"That's odd. Did you ever find out why he did that?" Sanders queried.

"I asked Rebekah after he left if something was wrong and she just shrugged it off. It was like no big deal. She just ate her meal as if nothing had happened. I thought she might be embarrassed about it and didn't want to say anything in front of Tom."

"Did you ever get an answer?" asked Mahoney.

"I tried to get it out of her the next day when we had one of our daily conversations, but she just said that sometimes he gets moody. She said it really was a work emergency and he was probably distracted." Both detectives nodded as they took notes.

"The thing is," added Angela as she stood up once again to take things to her kitchen. "After that, we never did anything as couples. We even had a trip planned up to Pismo Beach for a day to play golf and walk the beach, but that never happened. It was almost as if Hunter was giving us a test drive and we failed."

"Do you think that Hunter King is capable of murder?" Mahoney asked looking down at his shoes. Angela hesitated before answering. She looked him directly in the eyes and said, "Yes I do."

Chapter 15

The detectives thanked Angela for her time, and she saw them to the door. They agreed to contact her should additional questions come up. She nodded but said nothing. As they walked to their separate cars, Mahoney seemed to be deep in thought.

"So what do you think about her story? Does it ring true? "asked Sanders as he got to his car. Both cars were parked on the street just a few houses down from the Demarco's. "Strange the way the rich people live, isn't it?"

Mahoney shoved his hands into his pants pocket. "Other than having the time and money to eat in overpriced restaurants and drive outrageously expensive cars, the rich are pretty much the same as the rest of us. What impressed me was how our victim seemed to run hot and cold. How does someone go from being such a good friend to nothing at all? Sounds odd to me."

"I don't know. My wife, I mean, my almost ex-wife, has had these love/hate relationships with her friends and I could never keep them straight. One day she is besties with Carly and the next she hates her. One night we have dinner plans with a couple and before I can take a shower and change my clothes, the dinner date is off. A fight over the phone caused all plans to be cancelled. Seems as if women like this kind of drama." The two men stopped at Sanders' car. Mahoney was parked a few cars up the street; street parking in this area was virtually impossible to find. "Anyway, boss, I need to get home and figure a few things out. I probably should just go ahead and sign those damn divorce papers."

"You do what you need to do, Sanders. We'll talk in the morning."

Sanders drove off to his home in Garden Grove trying to reflect on the meeting they just had with Angela Demarco. He found her attractive for an older woman, and she had that style that seemed to be common with women from New York. He once dated a Jewish girl from New York City, and he found her sense of humor delightful. She was pretty enough, but it was really her personality that turned him on. It didn't last long for a variety of reasons, but he enjoyed his time with her. One reason it didn't last was that Katie came along and swept him off his feet. Katie. Everything changed when he met the woman who would become his wife. She was stunning by everyone's standards: blonde, big blue eyes and a killer body. Even men who swore they preferred brunettes or women with curves turned to putty when they met her. She was very much aware of the power she had over men; this gave her a confidence that made her even more appealing.

She was the type who normally went after doctors and lawyers, not police officers who couldn't earn enough to keep her happy. Yet, she fell for him. They dated for less than a year and then she was the one who wanted to get married. "Let's get married and have a dozen kids," she said after just six months together. "We would make the most beautiful babies, wouldn't we?" Sanders felt that he needed more time to get to know the real Katie and he sensed that what they had wouldn't last for long. Yet his future wife was not willing to wait any longer and wanted to get married right away. So they married on the beaches of Kauai with a few of their closest friends and family. After several months of trying, it turned out that having kids wasn't a possibility. After that failure, the marriage went downhill. She started having affairs with men at work, the husbands of friends and even her doctor. Finding a man to be her lover was as easy as finding an apple at a produce store. Everyone was available.

There was some irony in this situation in that everyone knew that it was usually the police officer who had a stockpile of available women lined up, waiting and willing to be part of his harem. In his case, it was even more true because he was young and good-looking. His sandy colored hair and piercing green eyes rarely went unnoticed. Yet it was his beautiful blonde wife who ended up with a married doctor who left his wife of 12 years and three school-aged children to be with her. Now Katie was waiting for him to sign the papers in order to officially end their marriage.

What was it about women who could trade up in a marriage when things started to get difficult? Men were guilty of this too, but it was usually men who had a lot of money or fame. How often did you see an NBA star or an A-list celebrity with a plain Jane wife? Once they reached their peak of stardom, they traded her in just the way they would trade in an old car. Women did this too; not as much, but they did.

Sanders arrived home to an empty house. Their cat, Feathers, was sitting near the front door waiting for him. Katie decided to leave the cat to him after finding out that her doctor fiancé suffered from pet allergies. She also left a closet full of clothes that didn't quite fit the requirements of the new man in her life. Sanders had three large black garbage bags placed strategically next to the closet so when he finally got the energy, he would pack them up and send them to Goodwill.

He hated the quiet in the house, so he put the television on to a local news station. He also had a Sirius radio in the kitchen which was set to a country and western station. The sounds comforted him.

What was it about these women? They ended up with successful men in beautiful mansions with expensive clothes and then, at times, ended up at the wrong end of the divorce settlement. There was little or no love there. Not unlike his own marriage. Yet why would someone who appeared to be as well-educated as Rebekah King be attracted to someone like Hunter King? He could see it if she had been young, from a broken home, in need of a father figure to help her get by or if she were just someone who was into sugar daddies. Rebekah, at least from what Sanders could determine, was none of that. What was there about her that made her act this way and was it, perhaps, related to her death?

Chapter 16

Jessica got the green light to re-open the studio the following day. The police had collected the evidence they needed, and Spencer and Jake were anxious to get people back in the doors. "We can't stay closed forever," said Jake when he picked up the phone the last time she called. "It doesn't look good. What are people thinking anyway? That the murderer is still lurking somewhere in the building? Let's get this operation going again, Jess. Money is a- wasting here." Jessica nodded in accordance with what her boss was saying. It was time to get things rolling, although she knew in her heart that from now on this high-end luxury studio would have the stigma of being the place where a student was murdered. Already the networks were contacting her to do a story on it for the drama show 24 Hours or Dateline. What a sexy title: *The Yoga Murder.*

The teachers were driving her crazy asking when it would be okay to return. Most of them made their living teaching yoga or Pilates and even a few days off work took a toll on them. They had rent to pay and food to buy. If Jessica had been asked, which she hadn't, she would have suggested another four to five days before opening. People had short memories and something else gruesome would be in the news in a matter of time.

Everyone in her contact file was notified that the studio would be open shortly. She rewrote the email at least five times before settling on one version that didn't totally evade the issue but didn't dwell on it either. It just let everyone know that classes would resume at 7 a.m.

The Pilates teachers had to contact their private clients to see if they would be able to keep their appointments. Most of them agreed, but a few said they needed a break. This was tough, because the revenue they got from their Pilates studio was substantial and helped to pay the exorbitant rent they had each month. A private Pilates session with an experienced instructor was $90 per session in a package of ten. A duet (two people sharing a session) was $130, so having a busy Pilates studio was a good thing. Jessica hoped that in time people would forget that the studio was the place where a murder had been committed.

It was getting late, so Jessica decided to take a hot bath to try to relax before going to bed. She hadn't slept well at all the last few nights and fatigue was starting to creep in. She had no time to feel this exhausted and her past experience told her that too many sleepless nights resulted in a bad cold or a relentless migraine. She had to sleep, and pills were not an option. She slipped off her white cotton robe and tested the water with her toes. It was steaming hot just the way she liked it. She slowly lowered herself into the hot, bubbly water and hesitated, waiting just long enough to get used to the heat. Her long blonde hair was piled high on her head and she just let her entire body slip into the sudsy water. Heaven, she thought.

There were times when she wondered why she put up with all of this. She didn't have to work, at least not this hard. Her trust fund paid her more than enough to get by each month and getting by meant being able to afford her rent, her car and expensive dinners out with friends. Money was not a problem for her. Not working would also mean having the time to have a boyfriend or even a sex partner so she wouldn't feel so lonely all the time. It was true that the work kept her busy enough to not feel the empty loneliness Jessica would have felt in an easier job. Yet with a simpler job, she could date, meet new people and even belong to some sort of meet-up group where they discussed wine or gourmet cooking. The idea of not working appealed to her, but she also knew that it would just be a matter of time before she got bored. Jessica wasn't one to sit around and she knew that eventually this would all pass.

Her mom, still a stunner at nearly 60, was hoping that her only daughter would settle down and get married. She was even eager for a grandchild, which surprised Jessica because her mom was always one to shave several years off her age.

She had serious relationships in the past. There was that guy Nick from college who also came from money and privilege. He had the very same background as hers, only he was a Boston blue blood. He was madly in love with her, but at the time his love seemed more stifling than comforting. She looked him up on Facebook once to see that he was married to a lawyer and they had one child together. His family pictures were beautiful, and it wasn't without a twinge of envy that she scrolled through the photographs. That could have been her with a baby or two living in a big house with a manicured yard just outside of Boston. She remembered visiting him there one summer and thinking that she could live in New England as long as they could get away for the brutally cold winters.

After Nick, there was a dalliance with a slightly older man who owned several restaurants. He wasn't ready to get married, but he was demanding of her time and she had to be there whenever his heart desired. That also didn't work out for her.

So for the time being, she was perfectly content with her 1100 sq. foot Laguna Beach condo which was a gift from her father, her dog and her job at Newport Yoga and Pilates. Maybe after her birthday in August she would reconsider her life choices, but for now, she thought as she relaxed in the bath, everything was okay.

Chapter 17

Mahoney stopped by the local donut store to pick up a dozen donuts for the guys at the precinct. He knew they always appreciated the gesture and it helped to keep everything going on a more even keel. It was a very small price to pay for a healthier work environment, although the word *healthy* was a poor choice of words when talking about donuts. He patted his own belly before grabbing his favorite glazed donut from the box. He would keep the purchase a secret from his wife. She thought donuts were about the worst thing anyone could eat. He would look into going on a diet next week. That Keto diet sounded good, but how long could he really go without a bowl of vanilla ice cream or a morning donut? Not long, that was for sure. It was already hard enough giving up the beer. He was doing a good job of that but ask him to give up sweets and bread was just taking it too far.

Sanders wasn't in the office yet. He usually was there at the crack of dawn, well into his work by the time Mahoney rolled in with his box of donuts. Mahoney was well aware that his partner was going through a rough time, and he felt for him. He was blessed to be married to Lizzie and to have never experienced the pain of a broken marriage. They had their tough times, but what marriage didn't. He never cheated on her, for which he felt he deserved a medal. He was in a profession where cheating was as commonplace as free donuts. Something about the uniform drove women crazy. When he became a detective, it was no longer the uniform, but the concept of being someone who was responsible for solving crimes. NCIS and CSI made his profession sexy and the head detectives were able to figure out the crime within the 53 minutes airtime that the show was allotted, after commercials. In real life the detectives tended to have an extra 15 pounds, if not more, and the crimes took a lot longer to solve than the time slotted for a TV drama. Yet nearly everyone he knew stepped out on a spouse from time to time. Too darn much temptation.

Reflecting on the Rebekah King case, he felt strongly that either it was the husband who wanted that divorce quicker and cheaper than he had been advised or else it was she who was having an affair. A jealous wife? A jilted lover? Did she have the goods on someone and was getting ready to tell? Could it be a former friend who was hateful and jealous and felt this was what needed to be done? He didn't think it was a woman based on the strength required to strangle her quickly and efficiently, although one never knew nowadays. Women could be as strong as men.

As he was thinking through all the possibilities, Sanders walked in, looking less disheveled than he had the day before. He almost looked handsome. He was clean shaven, hair brushed, and his clothes were clean. Mahoney thought about making a comment about how well his partner cleaned up, but then thought better of it. Sanders was obviously trying harder to look the part. Best to let it be.

"Brought some donuts in this morning. Help yourself," said Mahoney, knowing full well that the younger man wouldn't touch them.

"Thanks, but nah. I'm trying to watch my figure." He patted his flat belly as he walked by Mahoney's desk glancing at the pile of paperwork. "Anything new?" He asked as he hesitated near the desk.

"Just reviewing my notes," Mahoney answered without looking up. "I think we need to talk to Jessica." He looked up at his partner and smiled. "You've got a crush on her don't you? I don't blame you. She's very attractive." He tilted his head as he waited for a response. "I think she may be a bit too attractive for the likes of you."

"I agree," said Sanders. "Far too attractive for the likes of me. So why don't you go see her as I'm sure she has the hots for you."

"Right. I'm sure she is into fat old men, but in the meantime, she has access to all the clients and instructors at the studio. She also knows what happened at the party the night of the murder. To me that sounds like a good reason to pay her a visit and get some names and numbers."

"Yep," said Sanders running a hand through his hair. "Let's go pay her a visit".

Chapter 18

Sanders offered to drive to the studio; he had the relatively new Audi sedan that his wife left behind. He felt it was a slightly pretentious car given his income and lifestyle, but he enjoyed the ride. He knew that eventually he would have to trade it in for something more practical and a lot cheaper to insure, but for the time being he was enjoying it.

"Looks like the divorce did you good," Mahoney said as he climbed into the car. He wasn't usually impressed by vehicles, but this one was an exception. The dashboard had all the bells and whistles and the leather seats felt like butter. And it still had that new car smell. Mahoney felt a twinge of envy but then remembered that his partner was also going through a very painful divorce and this extraordinary car could not make up for that. He preferred his 2014 Ford Explorer and solid marriage over what his friend was struggling through.

"She left it. The boyfriend gave her a Mercedes coupe and she thought leaving this for me was a sign of her kindness and generosity," he said with a strong note of irony. "She does look good driving the Mercedes, I'll give her that." He put a bit more pressure on the gas.

They headed down The Pacific Coast Highway. They passed high-end car dealers, multi-million-dollar mansions, and expensive boutiques that had items only the very wealthy could afford. The gourmet dog treats at the local organic dog food store cost as much as bag of groceries. The ocean was calm today, making it difficult for the surfers to get their daily fix. They passed a group of cyclists in colorful garb who rode dangerously close to car lanes. Sanders had to swerve to miss them and one of the riders gave him a dirty look. "Damn bikes," he said. "They think they own the road."

"Well I'll be. I would have pinned you as someone who likes to put on tight neon shirts and ride with a pack on Saturday mornings," Mahoney said with a smirk. "You know, driving an Audi, riding your $3000 bike down PCH and next thing we know you're signing up for Pilates classes." Sanders rolled his eyes at the comment.

"What is the difference between yoga and Pilates anyway?" Mahoney asked. "I mean isn't yoga all that Indian and religious stuff? I remember dating a girl back in the '80s who was all into yoga. She was an odd one, but back then I wasn't all that particular about who I dated. She was very limber if I remember correctly." Sanders laughed. He wasn't interested in hearing about his partner's love life 30-plus years ago.

"I don't know all that much about Pilates other than they use these strange machines. Katie, my wife, or ex-wife used to take Pilates at a gym near our house. She swore by it and since she always looked so amazing, I figured it must work." He hesitated and tapped the steering wheel a few times. "But then again, she always looked good. She worked out all the time and ate very little. She never had that belly bulge that so many women get after 30." It was Mahoney's turn to laugh. Lizzie had the belly bulge, but it didn't bother him in the least. He thought it was strange that so many women worried about these things. His Lizzie was still beautiful to him and he was glad she had better things to do than work out three hours a day to look like a movie star.

They pulled up to the studio and found a parking spot very close to the steps. The lot was not full at this hour, but that had more to do with the murder that had been committed there just a few days ago rather than the time. Mahoney, despite not being an expert on fitness trends, knew that most classes of this nature started early in the morning and then again later in the afternoon. There were about a dozen cars in the lot, which meant that people were not yet ready to return.

They walked up the steep stairs. Sanders kept up a good pace, but Mahoney became acutely aware of the age difference, not to mention the different level of fitness as he trudged up the stairs. "Guess you gotta be in shape to do this stuff, "he said, trying to catch his breath. "I thought yoga was supposed to be easy."

When they got to the top of the steps and opened the doors, they saw Jessica sitting at the reception desk talking on the phone to someone. She gestured for them to come in. There were two women who appeared to be instructors waiting by the desk, drinking tea. One of them asked the gentlemen if they cared for a cup of hot tea or a bottle of water. Coffee wasn't offered as an option. Each man accepted the offer of water. The younger of the two women walked away without saying much, just mumbling something under her breath, and she didn't seem happy. The men glanced at her as she walked down the long hall to the back of the studio.

"Good morning gentlemen," said Jessica raising a single brow. "I see that Gina is getting you some water. Oh, and don't mind Leesa. She's angry about this whole thing. The classes have been beyond slow lately and having the police pop by isn't helping." She got up and motioned for them to follow her down the hall. They passed Leesa who had ducked into a larger classroom where there were three or four people waiting, presumably students.

"We'll go into this smaller classroom," Jessica said holding the door open for them. Both men were impressed by her professionalism. They had met her only the one time and she, with good reason, had been visibly upset and not nearly as polished. She was a very pretty young woman who represented the Orange County ideal in many ways. Her hair and make-up were flawless, her skin glowed and her posture was perfect. She was also dressed to work. Instead of wearing yoga pants and a top, she had on a crisp white linen blouse and tailored black pants. Her long hair was wrapped into a bun. Mahoney thought she looked a lot like the screen legend Grace Kelly in her prime.

She carried a couple of manila folders tucked under her arm. She rolled out three yoga mats and had all three of them sit on the floor. Sanders lowered himself down to the mat easily while Mahoney struggled. He narrowed his eyes at his younger and more limber partner.

"Please remove your shoes," said the manager calmly. "I should have had you do that at the front door. This will be our little secret." Sanders untied his shoes and placed them at the edge of the blue yoga mat. Mahoney tugged and pulled at his shoes and finally was able to get them off his feet. His effort made Jessica smile, but she didn't say anything. Most men coming to yoga did not wear leather oxfords and heavy socks. Rules were rules, however, and shoes were not allowed in the studio.

"We won't be here long, gentlemen," she said while thumbing through one of the files. "I know you're probably not accustomed to sitting barefoot on yoga mats on a hard floor," she glanced over at the older detective's blue and grey striped socks. "So let's get this going and we can all get back to work."

She had a list of all the members at the studio for both yoga and Pilates. Alongside each name was a telephone number and a check mark indicating that these people either agreed to talk to the detectives or knew the victim in any way. More than half had checkmarks and the others were clearly on the do not call list. "So, gentlemen, if you promise me you will not call anyone who has specifically asked not to be called, I would appreciate it. I have a business to run here and I assured those who were not comfortable talking to you or had nothing of any interest to share with you that you would not bother them." She shut the folder and gave them both a stern look. "Do I have your promise?" Sanders nodded but Mahoney shifted his weight from a semi-crossed legged position to sitting with his legs sprawled out in front of him.

"Ms. Howard, you do realize that this is a murder investigation and as much as we truly want to abide by your request, we can't make those kinds of promises. For example, if someone we speak to points us in the direction of someone on that list who has asked not to be called, we may have to call. However, if you'd like, we will keep you abreast if this should happen," He then shifted his weight again to his knees and stood up awkwardly. Jessica noticed his discomfort and tried to think of a solution. She had forgotten that not everyone was comfortable sitting cross legged on thin yoga mats.

She asked Gina to find a chair for the older detective. "You may want to register for a few classes when all this is over," she said smiling. "That way should the need arise for you to sit for an extended period of time on a yoga mat, you'll do it like a pro."

Sanders chuckled at that, but Mahoney just gave him a look. Not wanting to be the object of a joke he replied, "I'll give that some thought."

"Good," she said as she watched Gina bring him a folding chair. "And yes. If you feel the need to further investigate someone who has indicated they do not want to be contacted, please call me first. I would feel a lot better about it." She seemed anxious to get the meeting over and back to work. The owners were pressuring her to get the numbers up to where they were just a week ago. Many people had returned, but many had not and that was troubling. Having detectives hang around on a regular basis was also not a great way to get things back to the way they were.

Mahoney picked up on her restlessness and desire to have them leave, but he had more to say. "Is there anything else you can tell me that can help us with this investigation? Anything at all that you may have noticed the evening of the party or maybe before the party?" She tilted her head to the side as she thought this through. The last few days, that was all she thought about, trying to remember if anything happened that may be of interest to the detectives. She had not come up with anything that seemed relevant or important. At first it seemed like a challenge to find bits and pieces of the puzzle, as if she were playing a role in a detective show, but now it was just time consuming and frustrating. The only saving grace was the attractive younger detective who seemed to be noticing her too. Having a slight crush on Sanders made the investigation that much more tolerable. "Let me think it through and ask more questions," she said with confidence. "I am sure I'll think of something. Now, is there anything else?" Sanders also stood up as Mahoney told her that was all. "I am here if you need me," she said cheerfully, hoping that they would understand to call her only when necessary. She, more than anyone, wanted this case solved, but she didn't need the regular visits. The two detectives said their goodbyes.

"You like her, don't you?" Mahoney said, half teasing. He nudged Sanders in the waist with his elbow. "She is very pretty and very single, I think."

"She's okay. I guess. But I'm not in the market for a girlfriend thank you very much." He left it at that. He did find her attractive, but he felt at this point it was best to keep that to himself.

As they were leaving, a few very fit and attractive people were coming in carrying rolled yoga mats and wearing tight fitting clothes. The two detectives looked very much out of place

As they walked down the steep stairwell, Sanders was a few steps ahead of his partner, so he stopped and waited. "Well, that was helpful I guess," he said as Mahoney proceeded with caution down the stairs. "I think if we split up that list, we may find something."

"Maybe," said Mahoney. 'I'm just hoping that someone remembers something or someone from the party. Whoever it was came to the party or showed up later."

"It's the husband. It's always the husband," said Sanders mocking his partner as he reached the bottom of the stairs. Several more very attractive and fit people passed them on the way up the stairs. Sanders turned to watch a particularly attractive young Asian woman pass them, wearing black yoga pants and a dark green crop top.

"As I was saying," continued Mahoney as he gave a sideways glance at his partner, who was still eyeing the pretty young lady. "I have this feeling it may not be the husband and although it usually is, in this case something doesn't seem right to me."

Sanders turned his full attention to the older detective and stopped at the bottom of the stairs. "I think," he said plunging his hands into his jacket pockets, "we may find our answer on this list of names."

"Let's hope so," replied Mahoney. "Let's hope so."

Chapter 19

After stopping for another cup of coffee at an over-priced and over-trendy coffee shop on their way back to the office, the detectives noticed the relatively large crowd of people hanging around the coffee shop talking on their phones, working on their laptops or just talking to friends the old-fashioned way. Both men waited in line to order their $6 cups of fancy coffee as people ordered even fancier concoctions. "Do you ever wonder what these people do for a living?" Mahoney asked. "It's almost 11 a.m., so it's not lunch time and it's certainly late enough to have started work so why is it that this place is full?"

Sanders shrugged his shoulders. "I don't know. Times have changed since you were in your 20s and people now work remotely."

"I guess," Mahoney replied as he eased up to the counter to place his order. "It just seems that in a place where the median house price is over one million dollars and rents are over two thousand a month somebody somewhere should have a nine-to-five job. Wouldn't ya think?" He put his order in for a small cappuccino with just plain old regular milk which caused the barista to raise her brows. "I like milk from cows," he said to her as his partner rolled his eyes.

"Do you have to act like you were born in the 1800s?" Sanders whispered to his partner. "You know, you can be old and not act it." His partner shrugged.

After collecting their orders, they drove back to the office, immediately divvied up the files and got on their phones. It was close to noon, so most people would probably be available. As they had noticed in the coffee shop, people didn't work like they used to, anyway.

Mahoney got through a few names without much luck. He left two voicemails. One of the voicemails stated: *"Don't leave a message as I won't reply. Text me."* Mahoney replied with a text that said: *"Call me. This is Detective James Mahoney."* He figured that by brandishing the title of detective over this person, he would stand a better chance of getting a reply. Most people got nervous when receiving a call from a police officer or detective. *At least that was the way it used to be*, he thought.

His next call was to a woman named Sasha Clarke. He had heard that Sasha could be a man's or woman's name, so he waited to hear the answering voice. It was a woman. She picked up and answered with the soft accent of someone who originally hailed from the south but had lived in California long enough to lose most of the lilting accent. She sounded as if she was somewhere between the ages of 25 and 40, but it was always hard to tell.

"This is Sasha," she said in that sing-song manner that was common in the southeast.

"Hello Sasha," said the detective as he leaned back in his chair. He tried to picture her. The image that came up was a slender brunette with a long braid down her back and a clear, unblemished complexion. *What's going on here?* he wondered. This yoga stuff was really getting to him.

They talked for a few minutes, touching upon the case and then Mahoney asked her what he needed to know. "Sasha, do you have anything you could share with me regarding Ms. King, what she was like, and who she hung around with? Do you know of a few enemies she may have?" He cleared his throat. "I mean may have *had."* There was a brief silence on the other end and the detective could hear the laughter of young children in the background.

"Detective Mahoney," she finally said. "I would love to talk to you, but now is not a good time." Mahoney felt a deep let-down; He had a gut feeling that she had something interesting to tell him about the victim. It turned out he was right. "I do, however, have something to share with you. I don't know how relevant it is, but it's something I feel like you should know. Can we meet tomorrow morning after my 10 a.m. yoga class? There is a small coffee shop a block away from the studio and I can text you the location. I'll also text you a more definite time if that's okay with you."

"I would prefer that you come into the station," he said, making it sound more like a request than a demand. He didn't want to scare her away or make her think she was a suspect. He just didn't want to meet in a noisy coffee shop. He was tired of all the coffee shops that Sanders seemed to favor. She agreed, although she sounded a bit disappointed. He didn't blame her; being asked to come into a police station could frighten even the most innocent person.

After they agreed on a time and he hung up, Mahoney let out a huge sigh of relief. Finally, there was someone he could talk to who might have some information. He decided to keep this information to himself and meet with this woman alone. His partner had plenty of things he could be doing, including going down his own list and making the necessary calls. He was hoping that between the two of them and the list that Jessica had provided, they might get some answers to who and why someone murdered Rebekah King.

Chapter 20

Detective Sanders put down his phone after going through
five calls that produced no information at all. Nada. He left
two voicemails urgently requesting that the party call him
back as soon as possible and now, more than 24 hours later,
they had still not complied. He spoke with two women who
claimed they were very sorry to hear what happened, but
they didn't have an inkling as to who this woman was. They
both admitted that they may have seen her in class, but the
name did not ring a bell. From the sound of their voices,
both of them were a lot younger than the victim, so it was
possible they went to different classes at different times. He
assumed that the over-40 crowd preferred gentler classes
while the younger ones were more into athletic classes. The
last person he spoke with was a little bit more helpful, but
not much. It was a man who, by the sound of his voice, was
early middle-aged and still working a real job. Sanders was
surprised by the few calls he did make how few people had
what he considered to be "real" jobs. Some of them worked
from home, others worked from time to time and some
barely worked at all. Maybe Mahoney was right. People
didn't seem to work much these days yet were not lacking in
funds. It was very different from his lifestyle, but probably

more in tune with the crowd his soon-to-be ex-wife belonged to.

The man in question was an avid Pilates client and booked two or three private sessions a week with the same instructor that Rebekah had. Sanders made a mental note to call this instructor, wondering why he hadn't thought of that sooner. The client explained that although he technically never knew Ms. King, for a while his session was scheduled directly after hers. "For about three months I had an appointment with Kim every Monday and Wednesday at 8 am. Sometimes I got there a few minutes early, as you can never tell with Newport traffic and the bottleneck that seems to always be the case on PCH going through Corona Del Mar. Anyway, the few times when traffic was light and I got there ten minutes or so early, I would sit back, check voicemails and texts while I waited for Kim to finish with her client."

"Did you ever overhear their conversations?" asked the detective.

"Not really. I don't tend to listen to gossip and that's usually what goes on in these sessions. The women seem to get a work-out despite all the chit-chat, but I always find it distracting in my own sessions. However," he added, causing Sanders to perk up, "the last few times I was there she was quieter than usual. Ms. King seemed depressed or out of sorts. I was so used to their usual chatter that it seemed strange to me. Kim is an excellent teacher and she knows her stuff, but she likes to talk and when she does, her teaching isn't as good. She gets easily distracted. When I work out with her, I tend to stay quiet and keep her focused on me and my workout." He took a deep breath and continued. "I know I must bore the crap out of her as I just want to work out and then leave. It's possible they talked more before I got there, but I got the distinct feeling that something was off. That's my two cents worth anyway. I know that isn't much, but maybe it's something," he said.

"So even though you didn't listen in on their conversations, you got the distinct feeling that something had changed. Is that right?"

The man on the other end of the line took a few seconds to answer. "Yes. That's right. It was the *lack* of talking that I noticed. Funny how that is."

"Was there anything at all you overheard that might help us in this investigation?" Sanders asked hopefully.

The client hesitated for a second and then said no. He agreed to let Sanders know if he thought of anything relevant. Sanders thanked him for the information and the time. He was glad he at least learned something.

So not all that long ago the victim was depressed or distracted and didn't want to talk as much as usual. That didn't really mean that much. People go through phases and everyone has down times, but maybe this was worth looking into. He glanced at the rest of the list and saw there were still several more names to go through. Before he did, however, he wanted to get in touch with Kim, the Pilates instructor, and realized he didn't have her number in his notes. He would have to call the studio and get it that way. He wondered why Jessica didn't mention Kim from the beginning. Why would she leave that out? A private instructor would be a key witness, yet he was just finding out about her. He picked up his cell phone and started for the door. He called the studio and someone whose voice he didn't recognize picked up. "I need to speak to Jessica Howard right away," he said hoping that a deep voice and a sense of urgency would get her to the phone immediately.

"Jessica isn't coming in to work until later," said the young woman. "This is Gina, the assistant manager. Can I help you?" Sanders remembered Gina from the other day.

"No. That's okay. Please just leave her a message that Detective Martin Sanders called, and in the meantime, I'll try to reach her."

Sanders hurried out of the station office to his car, not wanting to waste any time. It was colder today, with a chilly and dry Santa Ana wind blowing in his direction. He figured he would drive around for a while and wait for Jessica to return his call. He could always think better when driving, and he needed to get out of his small, cramped office anyway. He decided to call the studio again and be more insistent this time. "This is detective Sanders and I need to speak with Ms. Howard right away," he said raising and deepening his voice making him sound more intimidating. 'Please have her call me on my cell or give me her cell so I can call her. This is urgent." There was silence on the other end. He pulled out his fob and opened the car doors. He got in and waited to start the car.

"I'm sorry sir, but I cannot give you her personal information. I will text her now and tell her to call you immediately. We are not allowed to give out that information." Sanders agreed but insisted that she get ahold of Jessica as soon as possible and to have her call him back right away. It was obvious that they played by the rules, but in this case, it was making his job that much harder.

As he waited for her call, he drove by the house where his ex-wife lived, on a hillside overlooking the Newport Harbor. He knew her address from the divorce documents and he had been curious about her new home. It was a cute white cottage with a pretty rose garden in front. There were two Mexican gardeners working as he drove by slowly. He knew that Katie would not put in the amount of time required to have a manicured garden. She had tried a few times at their house in Garden Grove but failed miserably. She didn't have the patience for working a garden. A late model Lexus SUV was parked in front, so she had either traded in the sports car or this was her fiancé's mode of transportation. He was tempted to stop and get a better look, but he didn't want to take the chance. He thought about her with her slick new boyfriend and his big spending habits and he could see, just for a second, why someone could experience enough rage to actually kill their spouse. He would never do it, but he understood the rage.

Sanders decided to start heading home and maybe stop at a French bakery that he liked to pick up some good bread to have for dinner. As he turned around to head in the opposite direction, his phone rang. He had shoved the phone into his pocket, so he had to pull over to get it out.

"I understand you need to talk to me," said Jessica, sounding calm yet vaguely annoyed.

"Thank you for getting back to me." He waited for her to say something, but there was quiet on the other end of the line. "I need to get in touch with one of the Pilates instructors who worked with Ms. King. Kim, I believe is her name." For a second, he visualized the pretty manager on the other end of the phone and he felt his cheeks burning. Thank goodness his partner wasn't in the car with him, he would have noticed it immediately. "I think she might be able to help us." He cleared his throat. "Why didn't you mention her before? She was Rebekah's trainer and therefore someone we need to talk to." There was silence and then a sigh on the other end of the phone.

"You realize just how busy I am right now, and this investigation is not my highest priority." She said angrily. "I have to run this studio, make sure everyone is happy, and now I need to help you find a murderer." Sanders smiled. She was right. This wasn't really her job, but she did need to cooperate, even if meant more work. "I was hoping that tonight I could review the schedule and see if there was anything or anyone that could be of interest to you," she added her voice softening.

"I understand. I really do, but I need to get ahold of Kim and talk to her as soon as possible. She might know something that could help us in the investigation. He pulled onto PCH going in the direction of the studio just in case he could schedule something within the next few hours. The French bakery would have to wait. This was more important.

"Let me check the on-line schedule to see when she will be at the studio. You have to understand," she added with a note of frustration in her voice, "our teachers tend to have more than one job. There isn't enough work at one studio to pay all the bills and if you don't reach her, just leave her a message. I can also see here on the schedule that she is teaching a private this evening at 7 p.m. You may want to talk to her before or after depending on her availability." He was relieved that she didn't argue with him. At least she was being reasonable.

Sanders turned the car around and headed back to the office. He was willing to wait, but not that long. He stopped by a bakery and picked up a few rolls instead. He could have them with sliced turkey when he got home. There was no need for him to go to the studio at this time. He decided to park himself at a coffee shop. He picked a new one that was trying desperately to compete with Starbucks, and he situated himself at a table at the back of the shop. Mahoney would hate this place, he thought as he pulled out his laptop and got to work. Now he could work alone without Mahoney breathing down his neck or any of the distractions from the office.

Unlike his partner, he didn't mind the coffee shops with exorbitantly high-priced coffee drinks and millennials hopelessly tied to their cell phones. He wasn't much older than the millennials, and like them, he also grew up attached to a phone. He wasn't as educated or as environmentally correct as so many of them, but he could relate to their lifestyle choices more than Mahoney could.

He ordered something tall and cold instead of his usual cup of plain hot coffee. The venue wasn't crowded, so he returned to the four-top toward the back, which allowed him to work quietly. He was not good working in noisy settings and was easily distracted by people talking on their phones. As a detective and someone whose job it was to understand motive and culpability, he tended to listen in on conversations, learning more than he really wanted to about people. Women bitching about their boyfriends, or men talking about an annoying boss. This skill came in handy when trying to solve a crime, but otherwise it didn't serve him well at all.

As they called his name, "Saunders" for some odd reason, he got up to get his ice-cold drink. As he returned to his table his phone buzzed. He looked down to see a number he did not recognize with a 949-area code. He looked closer to see it was Kim. Her message said *"Call me now. I am free to talk. You have my number."*

Sanders looked around him to see if anyone was close enough to listen and fortunately, the coast was clear. A man and woman were seated not too far away, but both of them were engrossed in their phones. A single man was typing away on his laptop and a few people were hanging out by the check-out waiting for their drinks. He called her right back. She picked up after three rings.

"This is Kim," she said. She sounded very young.

"Hi Kim," he said in the calmest voice he could muster, given the nature of the call. "This is Detective Martin Sanders. Thank you for calling me. I have a few questions I need to ask you and I was hoping we could meet." There was a brief silence on the other end. Sanders tapped his fingers on the table waiting for her reply.

"Um…. I am sort of busy these days. I work at three different studios and I am pretty much booked for the next day or two. I can make some time on Saturday if that's okay?" Detective Sanders continued to tap his fingers on the table. Saturday was too late. He needed to talk to her sooner than that, but her tone expressed her true feelings on the meeting. She didn't want to do it. This was where he could learn from his more aggressive partner. Mahoney wouldn't stand for this. He'd have a tried-and-true technique for getting stubborn witnesses to come forward.

"Saturday is a bit too late," he said trying to lower his voice to make it sound serious. "I had later today or tomorrow in mind. As a matter of fact," he said finding the confidence to get this thing going. "I *need* to see you within the next 24 hours or else this impedes the investigation. Can you let the studios know that you can't be there? I am sure that Newport Yoga and Pilates would find it in their heart to let you meet with me."

"Okay," was all she said. "I'll find a sub for tonight. Let's meet at 6:15 this evening right after my 5 p.m. class at another studio in Huntington Beach. If it's okay with you, we can meet for a vegan meal at a place close by. That way I can still make it for an 8 p.m. private client." They agreed on the place she mentioned up the road in Huntington Beach. He promised it wouldn't take much more than an hour if that. He was hoping he could get enough information from her to jump start this investigation; so far there seemed to be a lot of dead ends. He was getting tired of all these coffee shops and meetings with fitness instructors. He wasn't even a fan of vegan food, but he was willing to make the sacrifice so he could discover what Kim might know. *Let's see what Rebekah King's personal Pilates instructor knew about her,* Sanders thought. He hoped it would be worth the time.

Chapter 21

Sasha Rubin was running late for her appointment with Detective Mahoney. She had never before met with a detective, not even that time she had to call the police in a domestic violence situation with a former live-in boyfriend. It had happened about 13 years ago, and it was handled by the police. It was the final straw in that relationship, and now that she was happily married to a high school physics teacher, she didn't think about it all that much. Fortunately, the boyfriend left southern California for Oregon or Washington after spending a few weeks in jail. She was just glad that chapter of her life was over.

She was nervous about the meeting mostly because she wasn't sure she could really help. It was true that she did know the victim and she knew her better than she let on during their brief conversation. She and Rebekah had been friends for several months until Rebekah started acting strange and ended up going her own way. Sasha wasn't used to having close female friends, and this was why she bonded so quickly with Rebekah King. There was at least 12 years difference in age between them, and Sasha was the mother of two school-aged children. Her husband wasn't wealthy, and his schoolteacher's salary was just enough to be able to afford a three-bedroom beach house in an older Newport Beach neighborhood. Rebekah was wealthy and glamorous and didn't have to worry about money all the time like Sasha did. Yet Sasha really enjoyed spending time with Rebekah, and she liked the fact that her new friend didn't have the personality of some of the other upper-class women at the studio. The steep monthly membership was tough on them, but Sasha's husband insisted that if it made her happy and kept her fit, it was worth the money. She loved yoga and enjoyed the occasional Pilates class.

She arrived at the police station about 15 minutes later than promised. She ran a hand through her fine light brown hair, trying in a vain attempt to boost the volume. She had prepared for the meeting by wearing just a touch of makeup and a long flowing skirt, cotton blouse and medium heeled ankle boots. She was late because she could not decide what was appropriate to wear to such a meeting. Did one dress up? Dress down? She decided on her favorite style of clothing, which was twenty-first century hippy.

The woman at the reception desk was stout and very masculine-looking with short brown hair and a face that looked like it never saw a make-up palette or brush. She did not look pleased to see the tall skinny girl walk into the precinct.

"Can I help you?" she said quickly in a gruff voice without making eye contact with the visitor.

"Hello," answered Sasha. "I am here to see a Detective Mahoney about the Rebekah..."

"Mahoney's down that way. Just go to the end of the hall and turn right. You'll find him." She went back to shuffling papers, avoiding any eye contact with the visitor. Sasha continued down the hallway slowly looking at the name tags on the doors. She found the detective in the last office on the right just as the grumpy lady had promised. He was leaning back in his chair reviewing some papers with great intent. She tapped on the door lightly and he looked up, surprised to see her.

"Come on in," he said, returning his chair to the upright position and putting down the file he had been reading. "You must be Sasha," he said with just a hint of question at the end of the sentence. She knew he was expecting her, and she knew she was late for the meeting, so she assumed that he had forgotten all about it. In reality, Mahoney's mental image of the woman was so different from what he saw standing at his office door that he was momentarily stunned. No long dark braid, rather, a reasonably attractive woman in her mid- to late 30s with short light brown hair and a slender frame. He made a mental note to lose the habit of painting pictures in his mind of what people might look like, as it seemed he wasn't very good at it.

"Hi there," she said with the same sultry voice she had used on the phone. "I apologize for being so late. I really don't have any good excuses other than I underestimated how long it would take me to get here," she said sitting down in the only available chair in the office. "I'll be honest," she continued. "I have never been involved in any way, shape, or form in a murder investigation, so I had no idea how to dress," she said waving her hand over her outfit. Mahoney smiled and shrugged.

"You look fine for a murder investigation," he said. "Most of the time we don't look like they do in Law & Order

SVU. In all honesty we don't have all the extra help to get ready for filming." They both laughed at his remark. "So let's get going here," Mahoney said, pulling out a notepad and pen. "In the meantime, can I get you any coffee or tea? Sue, down the hall, can bring us some if you'd like."

"Um, yes. That would be fine. Tea would be okay. I'm trying to give up coffee." Mahoney nodded, and picked up his office phone and asked someone to bring them tea and coffee. Sasha assumed that Sue was the grouchy woman at reception was the person he called.

"So Sasha," Mahoney started as he leaned back in his chair with his notepad in hand. "Tell me what you can about Ms. King. How long did you know her?"

Sasha sat poised in her chair looking every bit the student of yoga that she was. Her posture was perfect which made the detective painfully aware of how poor his own posture was. She thought for a second before answering. "Well, I knew her a short while. Not long really. We took a few classes together and, well, I'll be honest with you, the morning classes tended to get very cliquey." She spoke quickly and it was obvious from the slight tremor in her speech that she was feeling nervous. "Rebekah and I were always the ones to *not* be part of the various cliques, so we connected right away. One day we ended up going out to a juice bar after class. We then made a habit of doing that every Wednesday whenever possible and we often talked on the phone during the day. Let me add that Rebekah's lifestyle was very different from mine. I have two young school-aged children who still require a lot of my time. I also work ten or more hours a week, although lately it's been slow." She hesitated as if deciding how much she wanted to reveal. She remembered how shocked and frightened she was when she first heard the news about the murder. She had never known anyone who had been killed before. She hadn't had much contact with Rebekah for the past several months, but she still felt like she had lost a friend. Rebekah wasn't a best friend or even a close friend, but they had spent enough time together for her to feel a bit of closeness.

After they talked for a little while and the detective was able to get her to loosen up a bit, Sasha spoke more honestly about their short-lived friendship. He would have never labeled what they had going on a real friendship as it sounded a lot more like two lonely women trying to find solace with someone in more or less the same boat. They shared a love of yoga, they both lived in Newport Beach, but they came from different socio-economic backgrounds. Rebekah was wealthy, and Sasha was not. Mahoney didn't believe for a minute that there were any *poor* families anywhere near Newport Beach as the median house price was about a million dollars and poor people as a rule don't live in million-dollar homes. But on a coastal Orange County scale, she and her husband were considered lower middle class. He once read that the amount of money one needed to earn to live in one of the Beach Cities was $200,000 a year and even that was a stretch. Thank goodness he lived east of the 5 freeway.

It didn't sound like they did a lot together, not like the way Angela Demarco described her friendship with Rebekah. At least with Angela there were dinners out, regular telephone conversations and even a meeting of husbands, even if that hadn't gone so well. Yet he felt in his bones that Sasha was hiding something from him. He was usually good at getting people to relax and then open up, revealing things about the case that they either hadn't thought relevant or they were hiding for whatever reason. She was guarded, however, and it took some time to get her to talk. He just had that sneaking suspicion that she wasn't telling him everything. What was she hiding?

"So what did you guys talk about when you got together? You sound like you traveled in different circles, but you must have had something to talk about. Right?" At that moment, Sue walked in with a deep scowl on her face and slammed the tea and coffee on the detective's desk.

"Here," she said. "Next time, the coffee maker is just over there," she pointed down the hall. Mahoney rolled his eyes and grabbed his mug.

"Thanks Sue," he said. "Close the door if you don't mind." She left in a huff. Mahoney chuckled. "Sometimes you get stuck with a curmudgeon," he said picking the coffee mug off the table. "Sue is our resident grouch. So, tell me about your friendship with Ms. King. What was she like?"

Sasha tilted her head a bit to the side trying to figure out how to answer the question. Why was this so hard for her? What was it about Rebekah that made their relationship so complicated? She knew she had to tell him something, but what?

"All I can say, detective, is that when she was done with me, she was done with me. It's like one minute she liked me and the next minute I no longer existed." She picked up the tea, looked at it and put it back down on the table. "I have never been what one would call a popular girl, and I can count all my good friends on one hand and have a few fingers left over." She showed him her hand wiggling her fingers as if counting. "One day Rebekah just stopped talking to me. She was over me and I was never going to get an explanation. I was hurt, but I got over it. At my age, having a best buddy isn't all that high on my hit list."

"Your hit list?"

"Bad choice of words, sorry." She nervously picked up the mug of tea and took a sip. She made a face.

"Terrible tea, I know. It's all we got." He pointed his chin towards the door and in the direction of Sue. "So who do you think is capable of strangling Rebekah King? Is it anyone you know at the studio or did she tell you anything about her husband, Hunter King?"

Sasha shook her head and crossed her long legs. "I don't know anyone who would have enough rage to kill someone. I know people who might not have liked her much, but to kill her, I don't think so." She put down the mug of tea on the desk. "There is one thing you may not know," she said so quietly he could barely hear her. "Rebekah was married once before. She mentioned it once on the phone but didn't go into much detail. All I know is that they lived in a very nice area of LA and she left him to move to New York. Wait," she said. "I mean Boston. I think she said he was a doctor, but she never brought it up again. That's all I know." She shrugged her shoulders. "You probably already know all this, but I thought I'd mention it. Seemed strange that she didn't say much about it."

The detective nodded as she told him about the previous husband. He wouldn't let her know that this was the first time he heard about this. This was news to him, but he tried hard to hide his surprise. "Thank you, Sasha. This really helps. If you think of anything else, please don't hesitate to contact me," He stood up and she followed. He saw her to the door.

"Again, if you think of anything please call me right away."

"I will," she said. Then she hesitated for a second before saying, "I just don't get it. Why would anyone kill her?"

Chapter 22

Things were starting to get back to normal at Newport Yoga and Pilates. It was now almost a full week after the murder and people were finally ready to rejoin group classes. Not everyone dared to return to a place where a woman had been strangled and the murderer was still out there; however, many did trudge up the long staircase, having decided that the odds of being slain during a yoga flow class were slim to none. Even those who spent a small fortune to take private or semi-private Pilates classes in the very room where the woman was strangled to death were resuming their pre-paid sessions. Yet the murder remained unsolved, which was unsettling to Kim. She couldn't help but feel the presence of something dark and evil every time she set foot in the studio.

Tonight was her scheduled appointment with the younger detective on the case. She had seen both men at the studio talking to Jessica and she noticed the younger one because He was very good-looking. The older guy looked more like what a cop should look like: older, chubby, and not someone you would notice in a crowd. She had her morning classes at the Newport studio and she normally had two evening mat classes at a large gym in Huntington Beach.

She called them right away, telling them something urgent had come up and she needed a last-minute sub for her two back-to-back mat classes. She hated doing this because not only did she really enjoy the thrill of teaching a large group of students, but also the money was good and she needed the work. Meeting face-to-face with the detective, however, was something she had to do in order to help resolve this case. She wasn't sure just how much help she would be, but she couldn't be any worse than any of the other teachers. Kim knew she had the reputation among other Pilates instructors as being too cozy with the clients. She chalked it up to jealousy as she was busier and made more money than the others. However, they had a point. She did talk too much and ask too many questions and one day it might just bite her in the butt.

Before the meeting, Kim called her mother, who lived in Northern California in a small beach town just north of San Francisco. Her mom, who was in her early 50s and dating up a storm after a nasty divorce from her second husband, was fascinated by the case. She was an avid reader of mystery stories and loved watching true crime dramas on TV. "You must keep me posted," she said rushing out the door to meet someone new for lunch. "This may just do wonders for your career." Kim doubted that would be the case. As a matter of fact, when the topic came up during her private and semi-private sessions, she said very little. It seemed wrong to talk about it all with other clients. She knew that she was fortunate to even have as many clients as she had. The market for private Pilates was waning in Southern California due to the proliferation of large group classes that were more fun and a lot less expensive. Talking non-stop about a brutal murder that took place in this very room was not going to keep those numbers up; it would most likely have the opposite effect. As much as people liked a little drama now and again, this was much too close to home.

When someone asked her for detailed information about the murdered client, she said very little. No need to spread rumors that could impede the case. She just told the truth: she wasn't there when it happened. They often pleaded with her for details, but she just replied she didn't know any more than they did.

She searched her brain to remember if Rebekah had said anything to her during their sessions. Rebekah was hot and cold with her. Some days she was a real chatterbox, while other days she barely said two words. Several weeks before the murder, she was glowing as if she had just fallen in love, yet not but a week or two later she was quiet again. Kim had asked her if she was okay, but Rebekah just shrugged and continued to work out. Kim knew that something was up with her, but she had no idea what it was. At the time, she just chalked it up to being human. Women who took private Pilates sessions on a regular basis had the tendency to be moody. Maybe all women were this way, but it seemed to be more the case in Orange County. She knew she had to be honest and open with the young detective, and she was hoping to be able to deliver some good information. Maybe Rebekah's mood swings were just the thing he needed to know in order to help find the culprit. Whatever the outcome, she was looking forward to meeting the detective later that day.

Chapter 23

Kim arrived at Vegan Delights precisely eleven minutes before her scheduled appointment. Having never been to an interview with a detective, she didn't know what to do. Would she have time to eat something before he arrived, or should she wait and eat while he asked questions? She sat down at one of the picnic tables that looked out on busy Beach Boulevard and pulled her phone out of her purse to see if he had texted. Nothing. He was probably on his way. Her stomach began to rumble, and she wasn't sure if it came from a bad case of nerves or hunger. She hadn't eaten since noontime and she was used to eating often. She went in, ordered a vegan burger and fries and hoped she would be done before the detective showed up. Her order arrived and she went back to the picnic tables outside. She figured that this way they could at least get started and she could continue eating her meal. Ten minutes later, Sanders showed up wearing a pair of fashionable black jeans and a dark leather jacket. He walked past her as she tried to shove a fry into her mouth. Her mouth was too full to call out to him so she let him walk into the venue and she would send a quick text, letting him know where she was. She knew him from his meetings at the studio, but he couldn't possibly know her. It wasn't like she was the only twenty-something, physically fit woman wearing yoga clothes at the restaurant. She patted her dark hair and swiped some gloss across her lips before reaching for her phone. He was better looking than she remembered.

After she sent the text, he immediately walked out of the restaurant.

"How did you know it was me?" he asked, sitting down across from her. His green eyes were twinkling, and she felt herself blush. Kim may have been a successful and popular Pilates instructor, but she didn't have much confidence when it came to men – especially good-looking men. Her mother, who had the uncanny ability to meet men wherever she went despite being older than fifty, couldn't understand why her 26-year-old, physically fit daughter was having so much trouble. Kim had a boyfriend in high school who dumped her three days before graduation, leaving her dateless for the prom, and then she had two other semi-serious boyfriends in college. Neither of them worked out. As a dance and Spanish major, most of her classes were made up of women and gay men. After college, her job as a Pilates instructor was not all that conducive to meeting men either. Her clients were mostly women and the men who did book with her were always married.

"I saw you at the studio," she answered pushing her plate away. She suddenly felt self-conscious about eating in front of him.

"Go ahead and eat," he said pointing to her plate. "I'll go in and order something for myself and we can talk out here. Just give me a second." She nodded and went back to picking at her food. Suddenly that huge hunger she felt upon arrival was gone. She pushed her plate away again and waited for the detective to return. When he did, he carried a tray with a large order of fries and some sliced tomatoes.

"You're not eating," he said, nodding at her. "Go ahead, please finish. I don't want to eat alone."

She pulled her tray closer and continued to pick at her food.

"Kim, I wanted to meet with you mostly because I thought you might be able to shed some light on this investigation." He put a long skinny fry into his mouth and continued to talk as he chewed. "I'll be honest and tell you that I know very little about Pilates or even personal training for that matter, as you can probably see." He smiled at her as he flexed his biceps. "What I do know, or at least what I have heard from others, is that often trainers and their clients tend to form close relationships." He took a long hard look at her to see how she might react. "Was this the case with you and Ms. King? Did you develop a close personal relationship? Is there anything she may have told you that could help us solve this case?" Kim swallowed a large piece of vegan burger and tried not to choke. She took a sip of water, hoping it would force the burger down. He watched her intently and it made her even more nervous. She realized that his piercing green eyes and bad boy good looks were distracting her as she tried to focus.

"Yes and no," she answered once she could find her voice. "We talked a lot at first when she started with me..."

"When was that?" he interrupted. He put down his food and pulled out a notepad and pen and began writing.

"I don't know the exact date as I don't have my notes with me, but I do know it has been at least a year. I started with the studio about 15 or so months ago and she started a few months after that." She thought for a second before continuing. "I remember the first session with Rebekah. She knew a little something about Pilates as she had taken some sessions at another studio before moving down here, and she was pretty adamant about how she wanted me to teach." Detective Sanders was writing all this down.

"Go on," Sanders said. Just then two couples sat down next to them. They were talking loudly and laughing. The detective looked over at Kim and shook his head. "We may need to continue this conversation elsewhere," he said, glancing at his watch. "Don't you have something you need to be doing later this evening?"

"I have a class in a little while, but I think we can just move over there," she said pointing to a smaller table in the corner. "I think it may be better and quieter," she added, putting all the leftovers onto the plate to toss in the garbage.

They moved to the small table and continued their conversation. As it got later in the evening, more and more people showed up to order food. Vegan food was popular these days among millennials and older hippies.

"So you were telling me a little bit about your first sessions with Rebekah King before we were interrupted." He placed his tray of half-eaten food onto the table and glanced back at the people who caused them to move. "Please continue."

Kim went on to tell him how determined the victim was to be taught a certain way. She did not like the more

121

contemporary approach, which was becoming more and more popular in Orange County, to the point where most people had no idea what true Pilates was, not even the teachers. Kim explained that she got her initial training in Los Angeles with a well-established teacher in Brentwood and had a solid background in the real deal. "I worried a bit that no one would like my classes and that no one would ever hire me because the other teachers were all doing crap they either made up or came from other disciplines like yoga or boot camp." The detective listened to what she had to say but didn't know real Pilates from fake Pilates or even why it mattered. He listened and took notes, knowing that eventually this conversation would give him something he needed.

"Well, I did get hired at Newport Yoga and Pilates, and I do okay. Rebekah seemed to really like me, and she was such a good client that the studio started giving me more work."

"Tell me more about Rebekah," the detective urged.

"Sure. Like I said, we got along well, and she always put in a good word about me at the front desk. Anyway, maybe a month or six weeks after starting, she became more talkative and shared personal information with me. That isn't at all unusual with my clients as people can get very emotional when working out – especially one-on-one." Sanders raised a single brow. He couldn't imagine getting up close and personal with someone as they made you work out. He didn't have a lot of experience with trainers, but he knew he didn't like talking about himself with people he didn't know well. Women were different, he guessed.

"About a month before this happened, she started to talk a bit about her husband, I mean ex-husband, and what a terrible person he was." A busboy came by to clear their plates and asked if there was anything else they wanted. They both said no.

"Had she ever talked about her husband – I mean ex-husband before?" asked Sanders "You would think that the topic of – uhm - I dunno, rotten husbands, ex or otherwise, would come up in conversation," he said, thinking of his own wife and her conversations with friends and trainers. He was sure he came up all the time.

"Oh, you know how it is. She said she was getting a divorce and things were getting bitter. Real bitter," she said. "She also mentioned that she was dating but hadn't found anyone worth her while. She often mentioned that women her age had a harder time of it, but I told her that just wasn't true. My own mom is in her early fifties – a good eight years older than Rebekah - and she dates more than I do." Sanders laughed at that. He found it hard to believe, because the woman in front of him was very attractive and poised and he thought it was kind of sexy that she was a Pilates instructor, even if he didn't know a thing about it.

"So when she started to talk about her mean and evil soon to be ex, what did she tell you? Were they in touch? Did they ever go out together? What did she discuss with you?"

Kim went on to tell the detective what little she knew. She said that on some days she was chattier than others and, on some days, she came into her session looking tired and upset. On the days she came in looking grim, the conversations went nowhere. The instructor explained that usually clients talk more when they are angry or upset. "It's hard to get them to focus much, as all they want to do is talk." She shrugged. "I guess I'm cheaper than a shrink and they at least get a workout in when they see me."

Kim glanced at her phone and stood up quickly. It was a few minutes past seven. "I really should get going," she said as she put on her hoodie and zipped it up. A cold sea breeze was blowing, and the temperature had dropped a good ten degrees. "I have a class in a bit, and I tend to like to get there early so I can prepare myself. It's also another 20-minute drive, since there is a lot of traffic at this time." Detective Martin Sanders stood up with her.

"Thank you so much for your time," he said as he put his notepad into his jacket pocket. "I hope you don't mind if I call you again if any questions arise. Next time we can meet at my office if that's okay with you." She nodded her approval. She wouldn't mind a bit if he called again.

"Oh," she said as she started to leave. "There's something else I forgot to tell you." She took a few steps toward the small table where the detective was getting ready to leave. "There is something else," she repeated," taking a deep breath. "I didn't want to mention it as it seemed like such an invasion of privacy, but I really can't think that way anymore can I?I don't know this for a fact, but I think she was having an affair. She never said so much, but she made a few comments that led me to believe something was going on." Sanders stood up straighter upon hearing this. This was the kind of news he needed to go deeper into this case. So far, no one had really mentioned an affair.

"Go on," he replied. "Tell me what you do know."

"Honestly, I don't know much more. She just had that glow about her. You know the look right? The one people have when they first fall in love." She blushed, realizing she had been thinking about what an affair with this handsome detective would be like. She wondered if he noticed. "One morning during our session, I guess I suggested it had been some time since I had had -um- sex and she kind of laughed and said there was nothing like great sex to cheer you right up. It may not have meant anything at all, but it was the way she said it. She was just radiant like women get when they..."

"When they make love," he said carefully.

"Yes. Exactly. She had that look and her mood had picked up considerably."

Sanders nodded and thanked her for her help. She was correct: It sounded very much like Rebekah was involved with someone at that time.

"It was a while ago and I just sort of forgot it until now. I mean nothing wrong with sleeping with someone when you're single, right?" She shrugged and looked down at her shoes. Sanders smiled at her comment.

"Anyway, I do need to leave, and I hope I was of some help." She turned around and walked quickly toward the parking lot. Sanders wrote that information down. Talking to Kim turned out to be very much worth his while.

Chapter 24

1999
Boston, Massachusetts

Keith finally tracked Rebekah down. He had hired someone to find her and it didn't take much longer than three weeks to learn the truth: his wife had left the West Coast for Boston and he had no idea why. He was hurt, angry, and confused, because as far as he was concerned, their marriage was solid.

The day she packed up her things and left, he arrived home from work a little later than usual due to a difficult eye lift on an aging movie star who wasn't in the best of health. He was shocked to discover that his wife was gone. She left a note on the kitchen island that said: *"I'm leaving, took a few things from the closet and please don't try to find me. I wish you the best of luck. Rebekah."* He checked the closet where just a few things seemed to be missing, and then the bathroom cabinets where he discovered that her make-up bag was gone, but most of her cosmetic items were still organized in the drawers. He tried to remember whether they had argued recently, but nothing came to mind. She had kissed him good-bye that morning, said she'd see him for dinner, and now she had disappeared like a ghost.

He looked around and noticed how neat everything was. He was surprised. She was normally messy and that was something that always bothered him, but he rarely criticized her. She didn't hang up her clothes for days, left dishes in the sink, and when the cleaning lady couldn't come for her twice a week deep cleaning, the house looked neglected. Today everything looked in place which bothered him more than her sloppy nature. It was as if she had never existed.

He knew she had her moods and she had been in a bad one these past two weeks, but he couldn't do anything right for her. He knew she could have benefited from professional help, but she shrugged it off when he suggested it. As a medical professional, he knew when something was wrong, and he had the means to find the best doctor possible to treat her. Not only could they afford the best care, but he also knew a lot of people and was able to get appointments when the average person would have to wait months. She wanted nothing to do with mental healthcare. She insisted she was fine and that it was just the marriage that had her down.

He was convinced that she had been unhappy with his long hours and she frequently accused him of having affairs with his patients. He saw many of the rich and beautiful of Los Angeles' elite, but never had he strayed. He had many opportunities, but cheating was not in his DNA. He liked being married, and cheating was complicated. He also loved Rebekah and tried hard to prove that to her by taking her on pricey trips to exotic places, buying her expensive jewelry and taking time off from his busy schedule to meet her for lunch and afternoon sex. The wining, dining, and extra attention seemed to work for a while, and then it didn't. When she got into one of her moods, he made a point of working longer hours and meeting friends for drinks after work. He hated going home at these times, but he didn't know how else to handle it. Keith did best when he was busy. He thrived on routine and when things were not right at home, he stayed away. That was what his father used to do, and that was how he handled things. He felt deep in his heart that one way or another, they would get through this.

Then Rebekah was gone. It was almost a relief knowing that there was very little he could do now, and it was just a question of hearing from her or her attorney. She would want a nice settlement and they could work that out. Knowing why she left him the way she did was more important than the money at this point. He needed closure. He waited a week, then two weeks, and then, before he knew it, several months had gone by since she had left. He tried to trace her credit card actions to see if he could find where she was, but there were no charges made to the card. He figured she opened up a separate account before she left. He also knew that unlike so many of the wives of surgeons, she could get by on very little. He remembered fondly that she actually preferred buying her clothes at Target rather than Saks or Nordstrom's. He had to buy her the expensive clothes as gifts and then insist she wear them to special events where she would be seen by his friends and co-workers.

When she first went missing, he called the police, but they didn't take it seriously. Many people *disappeared* voluntarily when they were unhappy in a relationship. He knew that the police were probably assuming that was the case, that he was an abusive husband and she needed to get away. None of that was true. He was nothing but loving and caring, unlike so many other extraordinarily successful husbands. He had his pick of beautiful young women who would gladly take his wife's place in their 3.5-million-dollar home and drive her Range Rover. But that never interested him, an attitude which always came as a surprise to his fellow doctors. They all had a mistress or two on the side and their wives tolerated it as long as they got their hefty monthly allowances.

A week after her disappearance, the police made a half-hearted attempt to try to find her, and he consulted with his attorney to see what he should do. He realized that to continue with divorce proceedings, he would need to find her. Two months after her sudden departure, he hired a private investigator to track her down; this only took a week. It took several months more until she agreed to a divorce and she was amenable to the settlement he offered. Her husband felt he got off easy and was able to quickly wash his hands of her and the years they spent together. His practice grew and he became more successful than he ever dreamed. He eventually met and fell in love with another woman and they married. He had pretty much forgotten his first wife. That is, until she decided to return once again to Southern California.

Chapter 25

Hunter King felt a cold coming on. He rarely got colds these days, but when he did, they were brutal. He had suffered from a terrible bout of pneumonia a few years back and he would do anything not to repeat that experience. Two days in the hospital, a nasty course of antibiotics and an inability to get out of bed for days. So he decided to cancel his tennis game in the morning and take it easy so he could beat the cold before it got too bad. They could find someone to take his place without much trouble. There were plenty of 40-something self-made millionaires who would love to be part of this elite doubles team. So many younger men looking to schmooze with the Newport Beach elite. Tennis, a few beers and some new names for the golden contact list.

He realized his cold came from stress. Damn it, he thought as he got out of bed and searched for a box of tissues. All this crap going on about Rebekah and now the detectives were asking a lot of questions. He knew he was the chief suspect in the case, but so far they had no real evidence. In addition to all of the fallout generated by Rebekah's murder, his girlfriend was spending money like it was air and he was starting to get tired of her. Beautiful young women like her were a dime a dozen around Newport

Beach and he was feeling the urge to trade her in for a newer model. Maybe someone who enjoyed spending more time watching Netflix or swimming in the pool and less time shopping. However, it would have to wait until this investigation was over and he was feeling better. Despite his money and mansion, no woman wanted to go home with someone coughing and spewing all over the place.

As he lay in bed lamenting the fact that he was stuck at home, he tried to remember what it was about his ex-wife that really appealed to him. She had a pretty face back then and had a nice slender figure that he admired. He preferred longer and leaner women as opposed to the more muscular and athletic look that had become popular over the past fifteen years. Back then when they first met, he wanted someone to be not quite an equal, but close enough. He desired someone who was bright enough to engage in a good conversation, but submissive enough to let him be the boss. Rebekah was bright, funny and, to a certain extent, supportive. The sex was good too, and she was great at role playing, which he found sexy. She always looked good and he was proud to be seen with her, even when he was with his middle-aged friends and they had their 22-year-old bimbos hanging on their side. Rebekah could make anyone laugh and she was always quick on her feet. Every once in a while, one of his buddies would tap him on the shoulder and say how lucky he was to have her. He knew that, too.

Then it all changed. They had probably been together too long and that's why the problems began. She was always so irritated and cross with him, which zapped any joy he got from the marriage. She caught him that one time in an affair with an associate of his, a slender Asian girl who was on the hunt for a rich American husband. It meant very little to him, but she took issue and would not let him forget it. That hadn't been his first indiscretion, but she was so busy with her fitness classes, friends and projects that she never found out about the others. He got sloppy with that one girl.

Then there was the trip to Las Vegas that she insisted on taking with two friends. He didn't like either of those women; they were typical Orange County divorcees with chips on their shoulders as big as Texas. He referred to these women as man-hating drunks who slept with anyone willing and then told the entire world about it. Before his affair, she would have never planned a trip with women like that. They went for three days and she didn't even bother to send a quick text to let him know she was okay. No communication whatsoever.

After Vegas it was all downhill. He worked until late at the office and stopped for dinner somewhere in Corona Del Mar before coming home. She did her own thing and then she moved into the guest bedroom. The sex had stopped cold turkey. He assumed she was sleeping around, as some days she didn't come home at all. The marriage was over, and now it was just a matter of who got what. She was clever, which meant she would find a good forensic accountant who could find things that he preferred stay hidden. She had the money to hire one too, which meant he needed to figure something out before it came to that. He just needed to stay one step ahead of her.

His net worth was substantial, and he was willing to give her something to just get the divorce over with. He could easily afford to give her a few million upfront and then monthly payments of around $30,000 although he would fight tooth and nail to keep that amount down. What did she ever do for him? It had been a mistake to marry her in the first place; He should have known better.

She never used to care all that much about material things so the fact she was being difficult in the divorce settlement made him furious. She had even made fun of the women she knew who claimed they couldn't live on $50,000 a month and now she was demanding almost that much. Just like that, she changed. He knew from previous experience that divorce could bring out the worst in people, but he had never expected that from Rebekah. He was glad she was gone.

Chapter 26

Detective Mahoney reviewed his notes after his meeting with Sasha. Once he got over the disappointment of being so wrong about her appearance and personality, he realized that she had provided good information. His ability to visualize people sight unseen would need some work. Who was this mysterious Rebekah King who seemed to at the same time have a lot of friends and enemies? She was truly an enigma.

There was a pattern that he was starting to see. She made friends easily, came across as both carefree and endearing and then, out of the blue and for no apparent reason, she cut people out of her lives. Could this be the reason someone decided to kill her? Did she happen to piss off the wrong person? Then there was Hunter King. He had a motive in the way many ex-husbands did. Perhaps she was demanding a larger settlement than he was willing to give. Maybe she knew something about him that he didn't want to be made public. He also had opportunity. His house less than five miles from the yoga studio and he probably knew she was going to that party. He could have shown up later in the evening and hung around the area until he saw her. It doesn't, however, explain how he could have ended up in the Pilates studio. If he had been at the party, someone would have noticed him.

As he was trying to put his mish mash of thoughts into something cohesive, there was a knock on his office door. He looked up, thinking it was Sue coming by to give him a message in her surly way.

"Come in," he said with his head back down.

Sanders walked in with his hands in his pockets. Mahoney noticed that he was starting to look better each and every day. Gone was the two-day stubble and his hair was shiny and clean. "Got a sec?" he asked as he walked in.

"No, Sanders, I don't have a second. Let me finish this up and I'll be right with you," Sanders shrugged and placed his hand on the doorknob. "Just sit down and I'll be right with you," Mahoney said, making a grunting noise as he pushed through some papers.

"I'm not sure what you have to say, but I learned something from one of the yoga students." He picked up the pile of papers on his desk and shuffled through them. "I found out that our victim was married once before. Married to someone who lived in Los Angeles. Hunter King never mentioned this at all. We had no idea."

"Say what?" Sanders gave his partner an inquisitive look. "What are you talking about? You mean there was an ex-husband before there was Hunter King?"

Mahoney nodded. "That's exactly what I mean. So what did you come in here to tell me? I hope it's something worth my while," he said, trying to sound irritated although the almost imperceptible smile on his face gave him away.

"I think our victim may have been having an affair. Once we know more about it, I think we may find our answer."

136

Chapter 27

"Where did you find this out?" Mahoney looked up from the pile of papers on his desk. He was at full attention. Sanders felt a sudden rush of pride in having discovered this bit of information prior to anyone else. He tried to suppress his smile.

"I met with Rebekah's private trainer, and she seems to think that Rebekah was involved with someone." He didn't want to mention that Kim wasn't entirely sure this was the case, and now that Mahoney was really listening, he had to be careful with what he said.

"An affair?" Mahoney asked. "Do you happen to know with whom?"

"Not yet. No. Kim, her personal Pilates trainer said that Rebekah's demeanor had changed completely and she had mentioned something about how sex can really change the way a woman feels."

Mahoney raised his eyebrows then folded his arms. "It's not solid proof that something was going on, and maybe she had a crush on someone. Who knows? We need to look into that as a possibility and figure out who it was if anyone. In the meantime, I'd like to keep looking into the first ex-husband. Husbands always intrigue me," he said leaning back in his chair. "There seems to be a pattern here. I don't know if you have noticed, but there is a trail of people who our victim befriended and then dumped. She was indiscriminate. She dumped her friends and her husbands. She got just close enough to these people, brought them into her fold and then they were gone." Sanders nodded, slightly disappointed that Mahoney wasn't paying much attention to the suggestion there had been an affair. An affair could be key in solving the mystery.

"Let's talk about this over a pizza. Sound good to you?" Mahoney said. "I can call Lizzie and tell her I won't be home for dinner tonight. It was veggie surprise or some such thing anyway and I hate veggie surprise." He made a disgusted face and then began searching for his phone on the desk, finding it under some papers. "Pepperoni and mushrooms okay? It's on me," he added as he started to dial. Sanders nodded. He had been looking forward to a healthy salad from Luna Grill but he was the one who called the meeting so a greasy pizza would have to do.

"So," said Mahoney putting his phone back in his jacket pocket. "This teacher thinks that our victim was having a torrid affair. Did she know anything else?"

"Yes. She suspected that her client was involved with someone and that after a long dry spell, she was having sex again." Sanders crossed his legs and tilted his head to one side. "That would explain a lot anyway. We always thought it could be someone she was involved with."

"We really need more information on who this guy could be. See what you can do. In the meantime, we have this first husband that came out of nowhere that we need to also look into."

"I think we need to run up to LA and find this guy. He could be a gold mine of information."

"Or not," said Mahoney. "But you're right that we need to talk to this guy and find out what he knows and to see if he could also be a suspect." At that moment, a call came in from the front desk announcing the arrival of their pizza. Mahoney got up from his desk to get the pizza from the reception area. He returned a few minutes later carrying a large box and a bag that contained two soft drinks. Sanders shook his head. Next time he would request a vegetarian as a partner.

"One of us needs to research this first husband and then drive up to LA and find out more," Mahoney said as he grabbed a slice of pizza. He signaled with his chin for his partner to do the same. Sanders reluctantly grabbed a slice and put it on a paper plate.

"Now we have two ex-husbands who could potentially have a motive to get rid of the wife." He ate quickly nearly inhaling the slice of pizza on his plate. "I wonder about the first husband, and until we know more there isn't much to be said. It could have been years ago and any animosity towards her could be dead and buried. Yet," continued Mahoney, "we can't rule it out altogether until we know more about him."

Sanders toyed with the pizza on his plate and shook his head. "Then there was the 'affair.' We can't rule that out either."

Mahoney shrugged. "Maybe, but right now that's just a theory. We need more to go on. Keep your eyes and ears open." He grabbed another slice of pizza.

Sanders winced. His partner wasn't taking the claim seriously. He would prove him wrong.

"Anyway," Mahoney said wiping a speck of grease off his chin. "I do have some ideas that I want to bounce off you."

"Pray tell, boss." He was getting tired of the games.

Mahoney folded his arms and looked towards the ceiling. "I don't know about that guy King. He has motive." He looked up at his partner. "She was probably after him for more money and was making his life miserable, but did he have opportunity? Why would he be at the party? Someone would have noticed him. He wasn't a member and he would have stuck out like a sore thumb.

"I believe you told me that it's *always* the husband. Isn't that right?" Sanders said, suppressing a smile.

"If anyone ever tells you that it is always the husband, don't believe them." Mahoney chuckled and then took a napkin and wiped some of the grease off his face. "Although most of the time it is the husband. Just look at all the case files."

"Well now there are two husbands who can be potential suspects, so maybe it is the husband," Sanders replied as pushed the half- eaten slice of pizza away. "It just might not be the same husband we thought."

Mahoney stood up and walked over to the window. It was already getting dark and the parking lot was thinning out. He put his hands on his hips and stared out at the almost empty lot. "Maybe it's the first ex-husband, but we don't really know much about him now. Maybe it's someone else. A teacher? A friend? That pretty manager Jessica? I mean, someone did it and that someone was at the party, right?" Mahoney moved away from the window and started to pace around the small room. This is what he did when he was thinking. Sanders waited. He always had to wait. "I don't know who it was," he finally said. "but I think I know who it wasn't. I may be wrong about this and we are not throwing anyone out yet as a suspect. Husbands are still fair game."

"I agree. At this point we haven't ruled anyone out. Not yet anyway." Sanders said, standing up and heading towards the door. "I need to get going. Got some things to do before I get home. Call me tomorrow when you know what we are going to do about husband number one. I'll go up to LA with you if you need me. Otherwise, I have a few other things I want to look into."

"I'll keep you posted," said Mahoney as he went back to the paperwork on his desk.

Chapter 28

Jessica Howard was dreading the meeting scheduled with Spencer and Jake later that afternoon. They had finally returned home from their Caribbean vacation, and the clear blue water and warm sunshine did nothing whatsoever for their mood. They were both livid that a murder had occurred at their one Orange County studio, although Spencer was taking it far better than his partner. They spent a day back in Los Angeles in their Hollywood Hills home preparing for the onslaught of media coverage. Jessica had handled the bulk of it while her bosses snorkeled with the dolphins, but listening to the two of them, it would appear that they had handled the bulk of the work.

Now they were on their way to the studio, and she was trying to clean up any loose ends and get the information as organized as possible. She asked them if they wanted her to call in the detectives, but they both adamantly said no. Neither of them wanted to discuss anything with law enforcement until it was absolutely necessary. More importantly, they didn't want the detectives hanging around the studio when students were there. "It wasn't a good look", as Jake had said earlier that day.

When they showed up at the studio bronzed, fit and refreshed, she had to bite her tongue as she was tempted to say something sarcastic. She knew that was her job to remain both calm and optimistic. After all that was why they hired her, but she could have used some help trying to make things look better than they were.

Spencer gave her a big hug while Jake just nodded. She nodded back at him.

"So have we got things under control?" Spencer asked as he pulled out a chair. His husband leaned up against a wall with his arms crossed at his chest. He looked like he had been dragged out of bed to attend this meeting.

"Jake. Would you like me to get you a chair?" Jessica asked standing up to get an extra chair from the back.

"I'm good."

Spencer looked at Jessica and rolled his eyes. Jake was Jake. "I know you've been working your little tush off during our absence and I wanted you to know that Jake and I really appreciate it. You've done a good job of keeping things going despite..." he gestured towards the Pilates studio, "all that has happened during our absence. We are glad to see the attendance hasn't fallen too much with all of this, but we do need you to do your best to get this over and done with so we can get back to normal."

Jake snorted and said. "Wouldn't you know that we'd be the only studio in LA to have a dead body discovered right next to a reformer. Damn! This just can't be good." Jake took a deep breath and looked directly at Spencer who apparently was tired of hearing this. "A woman was strangled, for Christ's sake. Ugh! If you had half a brain, you'd shut this place down."

"Jake. Just stop will you? These things have a way of working themselves out. It just takes time." Spencer looked at Jessica and shook his head. She smiled. She knew this was the dynamic between the two of them.

"You know what they say," said Jake, striking a pose with hand firmly planted on his hip. "No such thing as bad publicity. So maybe we need to look at it that way." Spencer didn't bother answering. He turned his attention to Jessica.

"So Jess," he said lowering his voice. "who do you think did it? You know the people around here and you certainly know who was at the party and who it could have been. Right? So tell me who *you* think it is."

Jessica hesitated. She had no idea who it was, but Spencer was fishing for information, so to get him off her back, she needed to feed him something. Something that would satisfy him until he could meet with the detectives.

"I don't know for sure who it was, but I do believe that it was someone who either worked here as a teacher or a student. Possibly even her ex. But I don't recall seeing him during the course of the party." She stopped to reflect on who she saw that night. It was so crazy busy and noisy that the husband could have very well been there, and she would have never noticed. "He may have been there with her and I never noticed. We had a big turn-out and I was running around all night. There were lots of people there." The studio phone rang. "Excuse me, but I need to get back to work."

Both men stared at her. Their eyes were as wide as saucers. "Really?" said Jake turning to Spencer as if he had just heard the juiciest piece of gossip imaginable. "She thinks it could be someone from here?"

"She doesn't know who it was. Even the detectives are stumped. It could very well have been the husband or someone from the outside who managed to sneak in. Who knows?" Spencer tried to remain calm but he was starting to feel the pressure. If it had been someone who worked for them, it wouldn't bode well. On the other hand, once the murder investigation was solved, they could move on. Spencer and Jake had speculated that the ex-husband had followed Rebekah here, hid somewhere and then found her and kept her hidden, until everyone else was gone. It didn't make a lot of sense; How could he remain hidden in this studio without anyone noticing? Even if he had, how would he be able to ascertain that his ex-wife would be the very last to leave? That sort of thing only seemed to take place in murder mysteries.

Jessica was off the phone. She checked in a few students and then asked the assistant manager to take over for her as she walked back to her two bosses. "I don't know if it was someone from here, but it would be easier to understand" she said, eyeing a few students wandering in for a late afternoon yoga flow. She wasn't sure if they should be listening in on this conversation as it didn't create the atmosphere they were trying for. Her voice got softer and she indicated for them to come closer to the desk so the students would not be able to hear. "I think it's best you meet with the detectives. Share what you know or what you think you know. I will have that set up for you by tomorrow." She made a mental note of this. "Knowing them, it will be tomorrow. Do you mind driving back down here early enough to beat the traffic?" she asked.

They agreed to come the next day, asking if she could set up the meeting a bit later in the morning so they could get some things done in LA.

"If you don't mind," said Spencer, grabbing Jake by the arm. "I want to look around a bit and then go back into the empty studio to do some paperwork. I see the small studio is free until later today." Jessica told them that was fine, and she went back to greeting the students who were starting to gather in the front room. She was glad that meeting was over. Managing those two was way above her pay grade.

Several more students pushed into the waiting area hoping to get into the class. Declan Stevens was teaching which meant that there were a lot of women in the class. A few men straggled in carrying yoga mats, but most of the class was made up of women of all ages. Declan had the reputation of showing up a few minutes late, but everyone forgave him because he was so good. It drove all the other instructors crazy as they tended to be in class at least five minutes before the crowds came flowing in, hustling to find a spot on the floor for their yoga mats.

"This must be hard for you," said a yoga student in her late 40s, with long flowing gray hair. "I think you're doing a great job keeping everything together, but I imagine it isn't easy, is it?" She leaned in toward Jessica, who was busy reviewing names and entering them into the database. She knew that the student meant well, but she was also frustrated that she had to manage all of this and still keep a pleasant demeanor. The students were starting to complain, attendance was down and even one yoga teacher quit after learning the news. Finding subs wasn't easy and she was responsible for it all.

She gave the student her biggest smile and replied. "It's not easy, but we have it under control. The detectives will be here soon and they are doing a great job of narrowing down suspects. Enjoy your class today and let me know if there is anything else I can do." With that the woman walked off, purple and green yoga mat tucked firmly under her arm.

Jessica hadn't even had time to look at the numbers to see if they had gone down or if there had been a substantial number of membership cancellations. She figured that was exactly what Spencer and Jake were discussing in the smaller studio. It seemed that the classes were full, but she needed to see the numbers and then do a comparison.

The studio had a competitive monthly membership program which allowed members to take any group class they wanted as long as there was room. Private yoga and Pilates were extra, but members got a ten percent discount on all private packages, which was unique to this studio. It was the Pilates coordinator's idea to do this, and although the owners turned their noses up at this, it seemed to bring in more people. Lots of people wanted to do privates to either enhance their yoga practice or to be able to use the Pilates equipment. Even in this affluent community, people balked at the high price of private sessions. A single private Pilates session with a well-seasoned instructor was $95. A package price was a bit less and the ten percent discount for members made it even better.

She finished signing everyone into the beginner yoga class, and let out a sigh of relief. She looked at the sign-in sheet and saw that there were just 21 people signed up for

Declan's class — a good ten students fewer than normal. There was no guidebook on how to manage a homicide where the victim was murdered right after an anniversary celebration at the studio. This was the type of event that Dateline loved to cover as it helped to boost ratings: Who didn't want to cover a murder in affluent Newport Beach? Even better, the murder was at a yoga studio where all the beautiful people go. Perfect for network ratings, horrible for business.

She took the next hour or so while the class was being held to get things in order. It was moments like this when she almost felt that it might be better to cash in some of her trust fund and forget about work. She could go to late-night parties with the other trust-fund kids, shop at Southcoast Plaza until she literally dropped and pitch an umbrella at Laguna Beach and take a nap while listening to the melody of the ocean waves. Instead, she was obligated to manage the studio and help solve a murder. It was more than she had bargained for and way beyond her pay scale. It wasn't easy even before the murder took place, only then there weren't detectives marching up the stairs ready to ask a lot of questions. Round eyed yogis, blessed with privilege and time, gathered in groups asking one another if it was really safe to keep practicing here. Jessica felt that if she had to reassure them one more time she would run out of there and down the stairs so fast no one would even see her go. Yet despite all that she loved her work and she was determined to help clean up this mess.

Chapter 29

2002
Boston, Massachusetts

Boston was starting to lose its appeal. It was a lovely town, but it was starting to get dull. Rebekah loved the little big city feel of this New England town, along with the great Italian food they had in the North End, but the cons were starting to outweigh the pros. She had suffered through her first brutal winter and realized that snow and cold were highly overrated. Yes, the first week or so was pretty and refreshing, but by the third month of below freezing temperatures and endless snow, she longed for warmth and sunshine. She also felt that the people were not as friendly as she had originally thought. In the 15 months that she had lived there, she hadn't made a single friend. She had a few sex partners now and again, including her married boss at the agency. He was fun and sexy until he wasn't. She got tired of listening him whine about his prudish wife who refused to wear sexy lingerie or try something new in bed. He was also starting to take the romance a bit too seriously. She even grew to dislike the accent that she at first had found so charming. She never thought she'd see the day where she would crave warm sunshine and blue skies after so many years of living in Southern California. Yet, after just one long winter, she had her fill of four seasons. It was different, but nothing she cared to repeat. Seasons, she thought to herself, were highly overrated. The small apartment made her feel claustrophobic on those days where it rained and rained and she was stuck inside. It was charming and cozy at first, but later on it was crowded and uncomfortable. The simple pleasures of low maintenance living were starting to wear thin. It was time to go home to the West Coast.

She researched several possibilities. Seattle sounded nice, but she felt it might be a lot like Boston only with more hipsters and gray rainy days. She looked into San Francisco, but the city was falling apart due to the homeless problem. L. A. was out of the question, so she finally decided on Newport Beach, which in her mind was the Beverly Hills of Orange County. Ocean view homes, good dining options and an affluent population with enough diversity to keep it interesting. While Orange County did not have the cosmopolitan feel of Los Angeles, and it tended to lean Republican, she figured that these things were comparatively minor. She just needed to go home, yet, far enough away from her old life to go unnoticed. She could rent a small place near the beach and figure out everything else later on. It would only be a matter of time before she met someone who could offer the lifestyle that she thought she had abandoned. Living in the small, cramped Boston apartment made her realize that having money and material goods wasn't as unimportant as she previously had believed.

Working in an office from 9 to 5, trudging through the wet snow to get to work and then, coming home to a tiny apartment was far from glamorous. As much as she despised the thinly disguised materialism of West LA, she disliked the starving artist lifestyle even more.

She hated having to rely on men because it contradicted everything she believed deep in her soul, but it was the only way to make the changes she needed to make. She had reinvented herself before, and she was about to do it once again.

She started to pack her bags, called to give her landlord adequate notice and began to investigate life in Orange County, California.

Chapter 30

Angela Demarco was replanting some brightly colored annuals in her small but expertly designed garden. She spent a good deal of time weeding, fertilizing, and planting so that her garden was as colorful and inviting as the small gardens on her street. Everyone was out in their gardening gloves and hats enjoying the bright California sunshine and doing what they could to make their multi-million-dollar homes look even more dazzling. Mahoney thought of his own Lizzie, who tried to spend what little free time she had cleaning up the weeds and trying to keep up with the seasonal planting. He had no idea what she did out there, but he knew he liked the results. On a quiet spring Saturday afternoon, they could sit outside and enjoy the breezy sunshine and admire the rainbow of colors of the freshly planted flowers. He would sit back, kick up his feet and feel blessed to be able to live in a place where weather was rarely the enemy. Here in Corona Del Mar, a community made up of doctors, lawyers and successful businessmen and businesswomen, he felt an odd connection with their love of gardening.

Although she was expecting the detectives, Angela didn't look like she put much effort into the meeting. She was dressed in a pair of shorts and a yellow t-shirt that had seen better days.

The morning after the pizza meeting at the office, both Detectives Sanders and Mahoney decided a meeting with the former best friend would be in their best interest. In any event, it couldn't hurt.

"Ms. Demarco?" said detective Sanders, who, as Mahoney noticed, was starting to look better each and every day. His hair had recently been cut and the five o-clock shadow was gone.

"That's me," she said, not looking up from her weeding. A thick pile of green leaves lay at her side as she clipped away. The two detectives moved closer to her and waited for her to respond. She continued without speaking.

Sanders continued the conversation. "We contacted you early this morning saying we needed to discuss few things regarding Ms. Rebekah King. We're going to need a few minutes of your time so we would appreciate it if we could get started." She ignored the request and kept clipping away. She pushed a lock of hair off her forehead and wiped off the sweat. The sun was getting hotter with each passing minute. The sky was a clear bright blue and unlike most coastal days, there wasn't a breeze in the air. Both detectives were dressed in long pants, starched white shirts and blazers.

"Ms. Demarco," Mahoney piped in. "We just have a few questions to ask and then we will be on our way. I know you are busy, and we will do our best to get in and out of here as quickly as possible." She moved a few steps towards her porch and put down her tools. She wiped another bead of sweat off her forehead and, for the first time, addressed the two detectives.

"What do you want to ask me?" she asked making no attempt to hide her frustration. "I thought we had covered everything the last time you were here." She glanced at her watch then looked up. "I think that was just two or three days ago, so I'm not sure why you came back so soon." Detective Mahoney took a deep breath and glanced out of the corner of his eye at his partner. This was clearly not the same woman who met with them just days ago. Something had changed along the way.

"We may have some new information, and we thought that you would be a good person to talk to. Just for a few minutes if that's okay with you." She didn't argue but gave him a look that spoke volumes. "Would you mind if we get out of the hot sun and somewhere cooler? It's getting unbearable out here. Hard to think that just a few days ago we were wearing sweaters." She shrugged and gestured for them to follow her into the house. She picked up her tools and a few weeds that she had collected and opened the door with her gloves still on. "Come in," she said with no emotion in her voice. "It's a mess in here. My cleaning lady wasn't able to make it yesterday, and I didn't have the time to do it myself." She waved her hand in the air. "She has some sort of virus or something and I didn't want her around." She marched them over to the same table where she had answered their questions at their previous visit.

"Sit down," she ordered as she hovered over the two of them. "I have about ten minutes and then I need to get back to work on my garden before it gets too hot. Besides," she said, sitting down at the table. "I really don't know what more there is to say."

Mahoney wondered why she was reluctant to talk all of a sudden: Had someone gotten to her? Did she know more than she pretended to? Did she feel that her first meeting with them was enough to clear her name and then she wanted nothing more to do with the case? Mahoney felt it was the latter. She was so gracious when they first met. She had even baked and offered them cookies. There were no cookies and coffee this time. He had felt he could call on her anytime he had a question or two. He always appreciated witnesses who were willing to talk and then be available at the drop of a hat if something else should come up. In all his years, he felt he had a good sense on how people would react to questioning and how well they would cooperate. In this case, he got it all wrong. Why was she being so difficult? Was it the case or was something else going on in her life?

"We understand you are under time restraints," said Sanders, feeling the need to assert himself. He had been taking a back seat to his partner lately and it was starting to bother him. He knew he had a lot to learn from the older detective, but he also needed to play a role and not just be a quiet spectator. "We understand that Ms. King had been married before she married Hunter," he said, glancing at her to see how she would react to this information. She looked surprised. Mahoney realized that this could be the first she had heard of it.

She looked away toward her beautifully remodeled kitchen, tapping her fingers on the table. Mahoney couldn't tell if she was shocked or hurt by the information. As a former friend, she should have known there was an ex in the wings. Women talked about these kinds of things.

Angela shifted in her seat. She shook her head and sighed. "Honestly, I had no idea she was married before Hunter. She mentioned she spent some time in Boston working a job and trying out the East Coast for a change of pace, but she never said anything about a husband." She looked up at the two men and it was clear from the look on her face that she was hurt. "She told me she moved to Orange County from Boston after she grew tired of the long winters. Was he the real reason she left Boston?"

The two detectives looked at each other. She was unaware of the fact that the first husband lived in LA and not Boston. It was pretty clear that she wasn't lying.

"The first — well — who we think was the first husband was in LA and not Boston," said Sanders looking through his notes. "From what we have heard, this husband was or still is a doctor, and a prominent one at that."

"Geez," said Angela shaking her head. "Just like Rebekah to get a catch like that and then take off."

"Why do you say that?" asked Mahoney. "Is it possible he was abusive? Just because he did well doesn't mean it was a good marriage. Her marriage to King, from what I understand, was also not a good marriage, and he is also a man of means."

Angela nodded. She had traveled in these circles long enough to know that fame and fortune did not guarantee happiness.

"I didn't know about the first husband," she said so softly that Mahoney had to lean in to hear her. "I do know, however," she said looking right at them so there was no misunderstanding. "that she slept around. She never seemed to be lacking for male attention. I found it surprising and – well – shocking." she added, sounding almost vindictive. "We live in an area where beautiful well-kept women are a dime a dozen and these young guys have their pick, yet she always had *her* pick of sex partners. I never officially met any of them, mostly because she tended to keep them hidden, but it was an entourage of young handymen, a fireman and a few waiters from the places she liked to eat. They were always young, good looking and great in bed."

Mahoney blushed at the last description but kept going. "Why didn't you tell us this earlier?" he asked trying not to use a tone of voice that would offend her. She was on a roll now and he didn't want to jeopardize it. She shrugged. "I didn't think it mattered. Remember, we hadn't spoken in quite a while so anyone she was sleeping with back then is probably long out of the picture." The detectives nodded but said nothing.

"You said you didn't personally know any of these guys she slept with, but do you know anything about where they worked or where they might be now?" Mahoney pleaded. "It may be worth our while to talk to one of her – ahem – lovers to learn more about her." He leaned back and clasped his hands behind his neck. "You never know what may turn up. At least we can learn something about her character."

"You mean learn something about which positions she liked?" This time both men blushed. That wasn't what they meant, but they forced a laugh.

"Not that," said Sanders. "How long did her relationships last? Did she dump them or was it the other way around? Was she needy and demanding? Did she move from partner to partner and then try to humiliate the last guy in tow? These are the things we need to know. We are looking for motive."

Angela shrugged. She didn't have answers. Mahoney continued the line of questioning,

"Usually women talk about these things and..."

"Do they?" Angela glared at him. He obviously had struck a nerve.

"I think they do. Close friends. Actually, Angela, I think Rebekah was the type to let her friends know that she had suitors." Sanders rolled his eyes at the word "suitors" but said nothing. Mahoney continued. "I think it is highly possible that one of her *boyfriends,* for lack of a better word, was angry with her about something and in his mind had a motive to kill her. I think if we could narrow this field, we may to be able to find who did it."

"Okay. I understand. At one time I suspected she had her eye on my Tom," she said gliding a hand through her dark hair. "I don't think anything ever happened, but she certainly tried." She looked down at her shoes and the detectives waited for her to continue. "Tom isn't- or wasn't - the kind that would run off with a friend of mine, but you never know do you? I mean I trust him, but men are men and their egos need stroking." She looked squarely at the two men. "Among other things." The two detectives blushed once again.

"I venture to guess that this pass at Tom was what destroyed your friendship. Am I right?"

"You would think so wouldn't you? No it wasn't that. It was so subtle that I just convinced myself that it never really happened. I had a talk with Tom later on and he sort of pooh-poohed the whole thing." She looked back towards the kitchen to see if her husband may be down there and then said in a lowered voice. "Honestly, I think he knew it was a pass and he was flattered, but after that he didn't want to even see her around."

Ready to change the subject away from Angela's husband, Mahoney asked, "So, given that she made what appeared to be a pass at your husband, are you aware of anyone else? Even if you don't know the names, just where this person works or what he does. We can do the rest of the work."

She hesitated as if jogging her memory as to who and when her former friend had been intimate with. Sanders knew that his own soon-to-be ex-wife would know exactly whom her friends were sleeping with. She would not only know with whom, but also when also when and where. His personal experience with women was that they paid close attention to these matters and knew more than they would admit to.

"I don't really know names. She was very secretive about her sex life. I know there was a handyman that used to fix things around their house. I remember we were looking for a good handyman as the one we had used previously went to rehab for a long time and then disappeared. She was very reluctant to share hers with us." She laughed and shook her head at the memory. "I wanted him to fix a leaking faucet in our bathroom, not sleep with me. I never did see the appeal of being with a guy young enough to be my son. Ugh," she exclaimed indicating with her hands how she felt about this.

"Tell us more about her flirtation with your husband," Sanders asked, continuing to write in his book. "Can you remember when that was?"

She crossed her legs and tilted her head to the side. Mahoney sat stone faced as he waited for her to answer. Some young children were playing in the yard and there was the continual noise of a larger ball hitting the side of the house. Mahoney winced each time it hit.

"The neighbor kids," Angela offered. "Dad is some high-priced attorney and makes a small fortune. I think they have about eight kids, all of them running around unsupervised." She sighed and glanced out the window as two towhead kids about four or five years old tossed a ball back and forth. A slightly older child had a tennis racket that she was swinging around, aiming at her younger twin brothers.

"What more can I tell you? It's all ancient history now. Rebekah didn't really start flirtations. She just pounced." She made a pouncing motion aiming towards Sanders and he jumped just slightly and then laughed. "That's what she did. She set her eyes on someone to satisfy whatever sick need she had to screw every man in sight and then she would attack."

"Please explain in more detail what she did to get their attention," Sanders asked. She glanced at her watch, reminding the two detectives that they were running out of time and she was getting tired of answering their questions. Sanders shifted uncomfortably in his chair. He wanted to get some answers in the short period of time they had remaining. "I know you are short on time, but if you can help us understand how she operated, this might help."

Angela looked down at her gardening shoes and picked something off her pants. She played with it for a few seconds before replying. The detectives weren't sure if she didn't have the answer or was afraid to say something.

"She didn't really do much of anything that I ever saw. I know with Tom," she turned her head towards the garage indicating his whereabouts with a lift of her chin, "she started to call him out of the blue. At first it was a text asking him how he was doing. He told me about it right away, thinking it was extremely odd that a friend of mine would be texting him in the middle of the day." She glanced in the direction of where her husband was and lowered her voice even though he wasn't within earshot. "Between us, I think he sort of enjoyed it. I trust him, and I trusted him then," she said. "He was just flattered because Rebekah had a sort of sex appeal that women didn't always see, but men did. Women always think that men prefer young blondes with big boobs and tight bodies, but sometimes just being willing and enthusiastic is all it takes to get a man interested." She looked at the detectives to see if she could illicit a reaction to what she said, but they remained silent and stone faced. "He told me right away that she had texted him and asked him to lunch over at Fashion Island. He was wondering if something was up between the two of us and maybe that's why she wanted to talk. I was confused because there wasn't anything up between us at all, and I had no idea why she was inviting him to an exclusive lunch." She shrugged. "He said he couldn't go as he had a meeting, but he didn't outright reject her so, I guess, she thought she could try again."

"What happened after he declined her offer for lunch? Did she call again?" Sanders asked, trying to find some logic in all of this. He thought back to his wife, and her indiscretions. She would schedule girlfriend weekends in Vegas or Phoenix, and he was too busy and wrapped up in his work to follow up on who was going. Besides, he wanted so badly to trust her, and he didn't want to be one of those guys who is always suspicious of his wife. She would always have her hair done and have a bikini wax and pedicure before she went, which he chalked up to something good-looking women just do before a weekend away. It turned out that the girlfriend thing was a ruse and she was meeting one of her married lovers for a weekend of illicit sex. He finally figured it out when he ran into one of her best friends at the local grocery store and he asked her why she wasn't on the trip. The surprised look on her face said it all.

"She called again," she said after thinking about it for a few seconds. "I don't exactly remember the circumstances, but she called him when I was away for a few days visiting my sister in Florida. Tom called me right away even though it was past midnight back East and he was pretty distraught. I guess the call took on a – how should I say – sexual tone and she invited him to a hotel room. Needless to say, gentlemen, that finally was the last straw in our friendship. Like I said earlier, it wasn't the initial flirtation, rather the overtly sexual call when she knew I was out of town that ended our friendship." The detectives took this all down. Mahoney had a puzzled look on his face. He was surprised how this former friend of the victim had started to open up. "Honestly, I never thought she was that kind of woman. I mean, I knew she liked to fool around, but never would she aggressively go after the husband of a friend." She moved forward in her chair and looked once again at her watch. She then stood up indicating that the meeting was ending." Let me also add before we finish that I was impressed with how Tom handled it. Not many men would have turned her down. There was something about her that really attracted a lot of men. What do they call that? Femme fatale? Anyway, I do need to get back to my gardening and Tom and I have a lunch date at noon so I'm afraid that's all the time I have." She walked into the kitchen and turned on the tap. "I hope I was able to help," she said sounding more like the woman they spoke to a few days ago and less like the angry person she was when they first arrived.

"Thank you for your time, Angela," said Mahoney as he stood up. "We will let you know if we have any other questions." Sanders stood up and walked toward the door. Mahoney followed behind. Angela Demarco nodded and showed them the door. She said a quick goodbye and then shut the door behind them. The detectives walked slowly down the stairs, their hands deep in their pants pockets. A brand-new Jaguar pulled up next to their car and an extremely handsome young man got out and ran over to the beautiful blonde children still playing n the yard. Daddy was home. Mahoney shook his head realizing just how picture perfect this place appeared to be with everyone rich, beautiful, and successful, but after years of working these cases, he knew that nothing was quite as perfect as it appeared to be. He took one last glance at the model husband and his towheaded children and then said to his partner, "You realize that there is more to this than we know, don't you?" Both men walked to their respective cars to head back to the office. They both felt that their meeting with the victim's former friend had provided some important information. Now it was time to put some of the pieces together.

Chapter 31

Mahoney arrived home to find Lizzy folding laundry on the kitchen table. She was still in her work clothes, and her shoulder-length hair was damp from the shower. She looked tired. "I saved you some of my vegetarian chili," she said pointing to the large pot on the stove. "it's a bit spicy, so make sure to pour yourself something to drink." She grabbed a thick bath towel from the basket and began to fold it.

"Hard day?" he asked, tossing his jacket on a chair and grabbing a stack of mail from the table to see if anything interesting had arrived. She put down the folded towel and placed her hands on her hips. "If you're waiting for me to serve you, you're going to be waiting a long time. And to answer your question, yes, it has been an awfully hard day," She walked towards the refrigerator and grabbed a seltzer water which she slammed down in front of him.

"I thought you said I needed…"

"I can get you a can of water," she said going back to the basket of clean unfolded clothes. "Yeah, it's been a totally shitty day. I guess there's this new flu out that is very contagious, and it is causing a lot of havoc at the hospital. Scary times," she said wiping a bead of sweat off her forehead. "I don't think people are yet aware of this flu as it hasn't hit the mainstream media quite yet. Be prepared."

He popped the lid off the icy cold can and took a sip. He would have preferred a cold beer to seltzer water, but he was determined to remain sober. He reminded himself that it had been too long since he had been to a meeting, and it was about time he found one close by. With all the pressure of this yet to be solved case, he wanted a good stiff drink more than ever. This was when going to meetings with like-minded souls would be a big help. He made a mental note of checking the AA website to find a meeting close by.

He put the heat on under the pot to reheat his dinner. He was wasn't hungry after the three slices of pizza, but he couldn't tell Lizzie about that; she would be furious. He had promised her that he was on what she called a 'clean eating' path. So far, he had failed miserably.

She put the last pair of folded socks into the basket and sat down next to him. "I'm just in a rotten mood. Sometimes I wonder why I even became a nurse." She sighed and looked down at her lap. Every once in a while, she questioned her choice of career. He knew she loved what she did, but it came with a price.

Mahoney reached for his wife's hand and squeezed it gently. "You had a harder day than I did. I just have to deal with mysterious murderers and unwilling witnesses. Nothing out of the ordinary." He took a spoonful of chili and blew on it as it was still steaming hot. "You, on the other hand, my dear, are in the face of danger each and every day. One can only imagine all the germs that circulate in a hospital. You're at risk every single day."

"Well that's what I signed up for, isn't it?" She stood up, walked over to the refrigerator and grabbed a beer for herself. She glanced up at her husband as if to say "sorry" as she still felt a bit awkward drinking in front of him. He shrugged it off. She then removed the cap and started to drink right from the bottle. "Besides, if I decided to retire, we'd have to live on your salary, wouldn't we?"

He smiled and shoveled some more of the hot chili into his mouth. "That would be a tragedy, wouldn't it? By the way, this chili is really good. Hot and spicy, just the way I like it," he said, shoveling another spoonful into his mouth.

Lizzie smiled and put the last piece of clean laundry into the basket. "Tell me about your day," she prompted watching him devour his meal. "Catch any criminals?" She liked to tease him about his line of work, but it was all in jest. She knew just how serious it was, and she was proud that her husband of so many years was doing such a good job as an investigator. She hadn't known if the working-class fellow she had married would be able to handle a job that required so much focus and brain work. It wasn't that she didn't believe he was smart enough; she just expected he would regret it later on. But she had been wrong about him, and she was glad of it.

"Nope. No criminals today," He pushed his empty bowl aside and squeezed the empty can before tossing it in the recycle can. "We just have this very perplexing murder, which is now being dubbed the yoga killing, where we don't have any real suspects. Not yet anyway."

"Is that unusual to be a few days into a case with no suspects?" she asked.

"Not really, but this is turning out to be a tough case." He sighed and shook his head. "Usually it's pretty cut and dried in these types of situations where you have a divorced couple with a lot of money and a lot of animosity between the two parties. This one, however, doesn't follow the usual pattern." He walked over to the refrigerator, looked at the few remaining beers and grabbed another can of seltzer water. "The husband doesn't seem to have motive, not one that we can find anyway, and although she wasn't greatly loved by many people, she wasn't hated either." He pulled the tab off the water, stared at it and shook his head. He missed his beer. "From what we can see she wasn't after a lot of money from her ex and she doesn't have much of a family that I know about, so I just don't know." He picked up the seltzer water and took a sip making a disgusted face. "Damn I miss my beer. I'm just too busy to attend a meeting these days," he said.

"Never too busy to attend a meeting, but you'll figure that out." She said quietly. "But back to the case, have you looked into her family? Is there an estranged sister or brother who stands to benefit from her death? What about her parents? I assume that given her age they are either elderly or have passed, but maybe there was money that had been distributed unfairly."

Her husband stopped to think it over. They hadn't given much thought to a birth family or siblings since none had come forward. He had just discovered that there was a first husband, and his Googling had resulted in a finding that he would follow up on the next day. It was a long time ago and the first husband didn't seem to have any motive, but it was worth looking into.

168

"You may be on to something," he said. "We haven't looked much into siblings or parents, but it's unlikely. Even if her parents are still alive, they'd be pretty old by now and wouldn't be all that in tune with her current lifestyle." But she was right; there were several stones unturned. There were also all these loose and jagged pieces that just weren't fitting together. He decided to tell her more about the case. "Turns out she was married once before. The guy still lives in Los Angeles and is a prestigious doctor. That's all I know. I looked him up on Google, but it took some time as I didn't yet have a name.

We found out about it from someone at the studio. It's criminal that we didn't think to look into this ourselves." He shook his head in disbelief. "I think we may want to look further into this doctor and see what he has to say. As a matter of fact, I am planning to drive up there tomorrow." He massaged his neck for a few seconds. He was feeling tight throughout his body due to all the stress, sitting and driving around. "The strange thing about our victim is that none of this seems to be following the storyline of a typical high society murder. I mean, it's almost always the husband, the boyfriend, the jealous ex-wife." He shook his head in disbelief. "Maybe it still is, but nothing so far seems to point to any of this."

"Was she having an affair during the marriage?" Lizzie asked, clearing the table. "Of course, if she were having sex with someone now, technically it can't be called an affair because she isn't – I mean – wasn't married. Assuming she was having a love affair, maybe her lover was married. Maybe her lover had a jealous wife or girlfriend." She sat back down and placed a hand on her husband's thigh. "Maybe, my love, this story *does* follow the storyline of a high society murder. You just have to look at it differently. For now, I suggest you go back to her best girlfriend and ask more questions. The girlfriends usually know. Now," she said moving her hand along his thigh. "I think it's time that we go upstairs and have a little *affair* ourselves."

Chapter 32

2000
Los Angeles, California

Dr. Keith Goldberg found the perfect six carat diamond ring that he was going to give to his girlfriend. Sarah was a nurse who had worked with him for years, and her inner calm, outer beauty and good nature were everything he desired in a partner. After a five-year marriage to Rebekah, he needed serenity in his life. He loved Rebekah, at least at first. She was feisty and sexual, but after she left, he realized there was so much about her that he didn't know. He learned the hard way what he wanted in a life partner, so he found someone very different from his first wife.

He had yet to tell Sarah everything about Rebekah as he wasn't sure how to break the news. She knew he had been married to a difficult woman who had run away from her beautiful West Coast home to move to Boston for no particular reason other than to get as far away from Southern California as possible without leaving the country. Sarah knew bits and pieces about her fiancé's first wife, but Keith never painted a complete picture. He just gave her the bare minimum. There were no children, the divorce was final so there really wasn't much more to say. She remained a mystery. What she didn't know was that he had to track her down in order to get her to sign the papers. It took him over a year and more than $100,000 in fees to find her. It wasn't a hardship to come up with the money for him since his practice was thriving, but it still made him angry. The divorce turned out to be a nightmare. Thank God they didn't have kids.

Keith Goldberg was eager to marry his girlfriend. Being single wasn't what it was cracked up to be. He preferred having someone to come home to, and Sarah was perfect. He had learned from his mistakes with his first wife.

His plan was to take her to dinner at one of LA's finest French restaurants this Saturday and propose to her there. This restaurant had a six-month waiting list to get in, but he knew both the chef and the owner and was able to get a table at the last minute. The owner had undergone a successful face lift two years earlier for which he was extremely grateful to the doctor. "Any time you want a seat in any of my bistros, all you need to do is call," he said, after the bandages came off. He kept his word.

The night went perfectly up until the time he asked her to marry him. She didn't answer right away, which made him feel nervous. He knew he was a good catch. Even with the 11-year age difference between the two of them, his success more than made up for his age. Sarah was a lovely girl with high cheekbones and thick auburn hair, but by Beverly Hills standards she was just average. He knew he could have his pick of beautiful young and engaging women, but he wasn't interested in perfect features; he wanted a soulmate and someone who wouldn't walk out on him. Someone who wouldn't move back East for no reason at all.

He had already planned and booked a long weekend in Avila Beach with a day trip for their engagement and he hated to have to cancel. If she didn't agree to the engagement, there was no point in making the trip. He had been looking forward to getting away and enjoying good wine and long walks on the beach.

She finally spoke up. "I love you, Keith, and I have for some time. But I am not ready to make the commitment to marry you. Not now." She took a sip of wine. "Maybe I feel I don't know you well enough yet. I wish I knew more about Rebekah and the reason she left. I feel that I haven't gotten the full story." She looked at him with her eyes wide. "Have you told me everything? Women just don't leave like that without a good reason."

This infuriated him. He had been looking forward to this evening for some time and he had been sure she would accept his proposal and they would leave the following weekend on their coastal road trip. Rebekah was causing him pain once again and there wasn't a damn thing he could do about it. He decided to leave things be and accept the fact that the wedding would be delayed.

"I understand your feelings," he said, pouring more wine into their glasses. "One day very soon I will tell you everything I know about Rebekah and our marriage. In the meantime, let's just make a toast to us and our future."

They went back to his house and made love until the wee hours of the morning, when he insisted on getting some sleep as he had surgery scheduled for that day. Sarah, more than anyone, realized the importance of a good night's sleep before surgery, so she wrapped her slender body around him and fell into a deep sleep. As she slept, the doctor remained awake. He was using the keen mind that got him through USC medical school and a residency in San Francisco to figure out how he was going to handle things with his first wife. Two hours later, he fell into a deep sleep without coming up with a single viable solution to this pressing problem.

Chapter 33

Keith Goldberg worked at a private plastic surgery clinic on a busy tree-lined Beverly Hills street. It was a small office where beautiful old mansions shared the landscape with office buildings made of green glass. Beverly Hills was just an hour-long drive on a good day from the precinct, but on this day, it took Mahoney well over ninety minutes to make the drive, park the car, and find the surgery center. It was hidden behind several tall oak trees, making it look more like an upscale condo development than a doctor's clinic. Expensive cars lined the street and beautiful women in designer clothes walked quickly to get to wherever they were going. Mahoney had to suppress a laugh, thinking how much this area looked exactly the way everyone thought it did. His relatives in Texas and Oklahoma would not believe how rich everyone was here in this small section of Los Angeles.

Mahoney spent as little time as possible in LA and only went when he absolutely had to. Whenever he did make the trip, he was amazed at how people lived. It was the same display of wealth and status in Newport Beach, but it just seemed more obvious in the wealthier sections of Los Angeles. He always expected to run into someone famous, but it never happened. Lizzie nagged him at times to go see a concert or eat at a top ten restaurant for a special occasion like an anniversary or birthday. Mahoney would argue that it wasn't worth driving the 405-freeway stuck in terrible traffic to eat or see something you could eat or see in Orange County. His wife had finally stopped trying and they only came to LA when driving through to get somewhere else.

He was able to track down Goldberg fairly easily. He wondered why Hunter King had never mentioned an ex-husband during their conversations, but perhaps he knew very little about it. He was starting to get the feeling that the victim kept a lot to herself.

After his search, Mahoney found a Keith Goldberg MD in Beverly Hills. There was no website and no Yelp review, just a phone number. There was some information on a medical listing that gave some basic bio information, which included where he got his undergraduate degree and medical degree. Instead of a headshot, there was a silhouette of a head – the kind one sees when a picture is not provided. He was either not very good at what he did or he did extremely well and only accepted the most prominent people as his clients. There were no specials, no two-for-ones and not even an address.

After trying a few different key words, Mahoney was able to learn more about the mysterious doctor. He was active in the community and had two teen-age sons, which made the detective believe that he re-married shortly after his time with Rebekah King. He found a picture of the doctor at a fund-raising event. The photo revealed an attractive middle-aged man with a head of thick white hair and a muscular build. He looked like a surgeon to the stars.

Mahoney's cell phone GPS took him to a parking lot just a few blocks from the surgery center. He walked to the center in less than five minutes and took the stairs to the second floor of the center, which had large glass windows. Dr. Goldberg's office took up most of the second floor. Mahoney walked in the door and was greeted at the front desk by a striking blonde who appeared to be about 35 years old. Her thick hair brushed her shoulders and her skin looked as if she advertised for a skincare line. She was stunning.

"Can I help you?" she asked with a slight Southern accent. A nurse came to the front desk and dropped off a few files and then said something to her about a new patient. Mahoney waited.

"I'm sorry about that," she said. "I guess you are the detective who's here to talk to Dr. Goldberg?" Mahoney nodded as she picked up the phone to let the doctor know that he was waiting. He stood patiently hoping to see whether the doctor would keep him waiting for a reasonable period of time. He never knew which it would be, but he had learned over the years that sometimes you just have to wait.

"He's finishing up with a patient," she said sweetly, putting down the phone. "He will be right with you."

"Thank you," said Mahoney, still standing, and hoping that there would not be time to sit down and get back up again. Each time he lowered himself into a chair, especially after a long drive, he was reminded of his aging back.

Maybe, thought, it wasn't a bad idea to look into taking a few yoga classes. Just a few minutes after the lovely receptionist put down the phone, Dr. Goldberg walked out with a 50ish woman who had a large bandage wrapped around her nose. The doctor looked exactly as he had on the website, only taller and better looking. Despite his age, which Mahoney calculated to be in the mid to late 50s range, he had smooth skin and sculpted features. Mahoney wondered if plastic surgeons hired other surgeons to make them look better for their clients.

"Another day of rest, Mickey," he said to the woman, who gave Mahoney a once over before leaving.

"Detective," he said extending a hand. "So glad you could make it. I'm Dr. Goldberg. Let's head to my office so we can have a little talk." He glanced at his Rolex and called out to the woman at the front desk. "Give me 15 minutes, Amber, and Hold my calls until then." He gestured for the detective to follow him to a small office in the back.

"Come on in and take a seat," he said, as he checked his watch. The doctor was serious about timing the meeting. The detective often met with successful and busy people and he tried to be respectful of their schedules, but in the case of a murder investigation, these meetings could take longer. Sometimes much longer. That was when detective Mahoney had to put on his cop hat.

"You are here, I presume, to discuss my relationship with Rebekah." He leaned back in his large leather chair and put his feet on the desk. Right away from the doctor's casual body language, the detective could see that the ex-husband was not the slightest bit nervous about the interview. In his experience, this didn't necessarily mean anything. "Shame about what happened to her."

Mahoney scanned the doctor's face to see if there were any tell-tale signs. Over the years he had a knack for seeing whether someone was telling the truth, lying, or hiding something. He could tell by their body language or the look in their eyes. Sometimes he got it wrong, but most of the time he was right.

"Yes, Doctor. We're here to discuss your ex-wife. I'm hoping you can be of some help. I know it's been a long time since she left you, but maybe you can shed some light on our investigation."

The doctor removed his long legs from the desk and sat up straight in his chair. He then placed his elbows on the desk and cupped his hands around his face. He looked to be in deep thought. "I haven't seen my ex-wife in a long time, but I would be happy to answer any questions."

"That's exactly what I need you from you. Please try and think back to your time together and let me know if you find something — anything - that could be relevant in this investigation. Anything at all," Mahoney repeated as he pulled his notepad out of his jacket pocket.

Dr. Goldberg seemed to relax a bit and began to speak. "I met Rebekah a long time ago. She was a very beautiful and sexy woman back in the day. She had what I used to call spunk." He smiled at the memory. "When we first met, I was just starting my practice here in LA and was off to a good start," he said, looking around the office at the symbols of success. There were pictures of him and his beautiful new wife in various places: Paris, Cairo, St. Bart's and looking tanned and happy on an African safari. Life had been good to him.

"Something must have gone wrong in paradise," said the detective, still writing in his book. "The marriage fell apart after just a few years. Am I right?" The doctor either didn't notice the sarcasm in the detective's voice or he didn't care. He smiled at the suggestion that something had gone wrong in what should have been a perfect union.

"Something was *very* wrong in our little paradise. That's true." His cell phone buzzed, and he looked down to see who was calling and then shoved it into the pocket of white coat. "Yes. Something was terribly wrong although at the time I had no idea. Let me rephrase that," he said. "I knew something was off and I did all I could to make Rebekah happy. You see, detective, nothing or no one could ever make Rebekah happy. All our money, the beautiful house in Pacific Palisades. The trips, the freedom to do as she pleased; it wasn't enough for her." He sighed and shook his head. "At first, I thought she was mysterious and I found that very sexy. But that same quality is what ultimately tore us apart. I had no idea who she was."

Mahoney scribbled all of this into his notepad. "Did you ever meet the family? The parents? Siblings? Friends?"

"I met her family once. We had a very simple wedding with a few of my friends and colleagues and her family never came. I thought that was odd at the time, but I was so in love with her that I didn't pursue it. Later on, we met her parents and her brother for dinner one night and they made some lame excuse for not being able to attend the wedding. I let it go," He said shaking his head. "There was some serious dysfunction in that family, but she refused to talk about it." He relaxed back in his leather chair and put his interlaced fingers in a thought-provoking gesture. "She had her good points," he added. "She had a wicked sense of humor. You don't realize how valuable that is in a person until you no longer have it." Mahoney realized he was probably talking about his current wife or someone else close to him. He continued. "She did wonders with the house and even did some of her own artwork. She had a talent for painting, but she never really pursued it. I liked her work. I liked it more than some of the expensive crap they sell at some of the LA galleries." The detective listened to the doctor explain his troubled marriage to the victim and wrote all this down in his book. This was a completely different picture of the victim, which confused him. In his experience over the years, people's opinions of victims didn't vary that much. This case was different.

"When she left, I was shocked. I had no idea she was that unhappy." His voice shook a bit as if he were holding back tears or anger. "We had our problems, but who doesn't after a few years of marriage? I worked a lot and I know she was bored and needed a hobby or a job, but I encouraged her to do something. She could have easily taken painting lessons, worked part-time in a boutique or office, or, hell, I even asked her to come do some work for me, but she wasn't interested. Then one night we got into this argument," He folded his arms and looked intently at the man across the desk from him. His calm demeanor took a dark turn. "She wanted to leave LA She had enough of the glitz and glamour which, of course, I represent. Who more than a celebrity plastic surgeon to keep the reputation of this town phony and shallow?" He shrugged. "I told her that I couldn't leave. I had built a strong practice in Beverly Hills and I had no intention of leaving. I knew she was unhappy, so I had even promised her a two-week vacation anywhere she wanted to go. I also told her she could travel without me if she wanted to. I trusted her to do the right thing, but none of that was enough. After the argument, I left the house. I went to visit a friend of mine just to talk things over as I needed a sounding board. We had a few drinks, a good talk and when I got home, she was gone."

"Did she leave a note explaining where or why?" asked the detective, looking up from his notes. "She made a quick getaway, so she must have left quite a bit behind, right?" The doctor nodded and then leaned back into the leather chair. He looked out his window at the streets of Beverly Hills, a view he must see every day of the week.

"I was shocked. She took two large suitcases and left everything else. Mind you, she had a huge walk-in closet that was filled with designer clothes, shoes and handbags and she left most of it. I finally gathered it all and gave it to Goodwill."

"Were you in contact at all while she was away? Did she call or write? I assume you found her eventually as you did manage to complete the divorce." At that moment, the beautiful young receptionist knocked on the door and opened it just wide enough to say "Dr. Goldberg? I hate to interrupt, but there's an important call for you."

"Yes. I am sorry detective, but I need to take this call. I have been waiting for it for quite some time. But to answer your question," He hesitated and looked towards the ceiling as if the answers were hidden in the beams. "She never called me. She never wrote to me either, but I was finally able to find her. She went to Boston of all places. She didn't want a divorce, but she didn't want to be married either. She wanted me to simply disappear."

"Well you must have gotten the divorce eventually as she was able to remarry - as were you."

"That's right," the doctor said with a trace of sadness in his voice. "We finalized the divorce about two years after she left. She moved to Newport Beach after just a year or two living in Boston." His phone rang again. "I'm sorry detective, we need to wrap this up and I need to take this call." He picked up his phone and with one hand over the mouthpiece he asked the receptionist to show the detective out. The interview was over. Mahoney put his hand up for a second to indicate that he had one more question to ask. The doctor, for the first time, showed his frustration and sighed deeply.

"Before I leave, I have one more question for you. Have you seen or met with Rebekah in the past few months?"

The doctor had the phone pressed to his ear. The friendly demeanor of before was gone. "No. I haven't seen her in many years." Mahoney detected that the doctor was not being entirely truthful with him. It was clear that the meeting was coming to an end.

At that very moment, the receptionist came into the office as a reminder that someone more important than the detective was waiting for his call. The doctor indicated with his chin that the detective would be leaving shortly. The meeting was finished.

Detective Mahoney closed his notebook and thanked the doctor for his time.

The receptionist waited patiently for the detective to gather his things and leave. She showed him to the door and escorted him out, smiling the entire time. Mahoney wondered if the doctor ever hired anyone who didn't have perfect features and a killer body. Probably not.

As he got into his car ready for the long drive home, he thought about what the doctor had shared with him. It was obviously an unhappy marriage, mostly because she wanted something more than he could provide. It seemed strange that someone as successful as Dr. Goldberg could not keep his wife happy. He didn't seem to be a cheater or an abuser, and he appeared to have loved his wife. What went wrong in that marriage and why was she so unhappy? He was beginning to see a common thread among all of her relationships. Both her marriages had ended and her friendships with women never lasted very long. Who was this woman and who was responsible for ending her life?

Chapter 34

Detectives Mahoney and Sanders pulled into the office parking lot at exactly the same time. Mahoney had just returned from his trip to LA and Sanders was coming in after doing some work from home. They got out of their cars and headed for the office. The morning had turned into one of those hot, dry days where the air conditioning is never strong enough and there is no relief from the relentless heat. Even the beaches were devoid of any breeze. Mahoney had spent a short time living in Georgia, and although the temperatures were much higher and the humidity unbearable, every public place and nearly every home had a good, solid air conditioning unit. Here, for some reason, people were reluctant to put an air conditioning unit in their in their homes, claiming that the sea breeze was all they needed. Maybe that was true twenty years ago, but it wasn't anymore. The precinct had air conditioning, but it was never cool enough, and everyone walked around fanning themselves with handmade fans.

"Looks like we decided to come into work exactly at the same time," said Mahoney, as he slammed the car door shut. "Where've you been? I'm just coming back from meeting with husband number 1." Sanders shrugged as he locked his car remotely.

"You'll have to fill me on the meeting with Dr. Goldberg. That had to be interesting." Mahoney nodded as they walked into the office together. Mahoney poured himself a cup of weak, lukewarm coffee and brought it back to his desk. Sanders was already there, going over his notes. "How do you drink that crap?" he asked as his partner dumped in two packets of sugar and one creamer. "Not only does it look more like tea than coffee, but it isn't even hot. Ugh!" He sat down and put his feet on the desk. Mahoney shot him an angry look.

"So give me the lowdown on the husband. Do you think he's involved?" Mahoney shook his head and sat down, placing the cup of lukewarm coffee on the desk.

"I don't think he is. I can't say for sure, but he seems like the kind of guy who gets his heart broken over a failed marriage. Not your typical rich doctor type," He leaned back and put his feet on the desk too. "The more I talk to people, the more I realize that Rebekah — may she rest in peace — was a very complicated and difficult woman. She's not like anyone I've ever met before. This case is not like anything I've worked before."

"So there was nothing incriminatory about him? No telltale signs?"

Mahoney shook his head and hesitated before speaking. Sanders was beginning to worry that this case would never be solved. Everything seemed to lead to a dead end.

"Right now I don't see a connection, but that doesn't rule him out. I'm not finished with him. Not yet."

Mahoney changed gears. He was done talking about Dr. Goldberg. "So what do you think about our meeting yesterday with Angela Demarco? She wasn't the same person we met the first time, was she?"

"No. She didn't seem at all happy about seeing us. She also had a motive. She was angry with Rebekah for chasing after her husband. I am certain she was also jealous of all the success Rebekah had with men. She made light of it, but I know that women get competitive when it comes to sex partners."

Mahoney scratched his head. He knew very little about women and their petty jealousies, but he didn't doubt his partner on this one. He had seen plenty of cases in the past where a jealous wife or girlfriend went ballistic when she found out her husband or boyfriend was cheating on her. "Maybe so," he said. "Yet I don't believe it was her. It was too long ago when this flirtation happened, and I don't think Angela is the type to show up at an event that she wasn't invited to late at night. Nope. I don't think it was her."

Sanders nodded. "I think she was having an affair at the time of the murder. Someone wanted to get back at her. I don't know who it was, and I doubt very much that anyone other than her lover knows," Sanders said. "On the other hand, someone may know more about the affair, which would ultimately lead us to her lover boy." The older detective paced behind his desk, holding the cup of rapidly cooling coffee, giving this some thought. He turned his back to his partner and looked out his window onto the parking lot. A few officers were huddled together laughing at something someone had said. They carried their lunches in bags and were heading into the station. Sometimes he missed the camaraderie that came with working with the guys. He liked Sanders well enough and the guy certainly had potential, but it wasn't the same.

"I wonder how much they know at the studio?" Sanders asked as he watched his partner gaze out the window. "In my experience, women like to talk about these things. They don't tell everyone unless, of course, they want their spouse to know. But they always tell someone. Men tend to keep these things to themselves. I mean, how many men do you know who discuss in detail what they do with their mistresses?" Mahoney shrugged and turned away from the window, then went back to his chair. He spilled the remains of his lukewarm coffee in the garbage pail next to his desk. "I wouldn't know. I never cheated. Not once, and I don't plan on it either. Ugh," He said slamming the coffee cup down on his desk. "Sanders, why didn't you warn me about this coffee? It's disgusting, and warm too." Sanders chuckled. His partner could be funny every once in a while.

"When your wife - I mean ex-wife - was having an affair, who did she tell? Did you ever find out about him prior to her asking for a divorce?" Mahoney knew something about his partner's divorce and the reason the marriage broke up. He knew there was an affair, but he never heard all the details. Like his partner had said earlier, men don't tend to talk about these things with other men. Especially two men in law enforcement. He wasn't all that interested in Sanders' marital woes, but he felt that it might lend some insight into this case. The scenarios were different, but they both involved cheating women who were appealing to a wide variety of men. Both women were high energy, attractive, and looking for more in life than their respective spouses could offer. Sanders' ex was younger and prettier than Rebekah King, but she was also more interested in moving up the social ladder. The victim had already accomplished that. In other words, she didn't appear to have money as a motive for having an affair. More importantly, Sanders' ex-wife was still alive.

Sanders remained quiet for a few seconds. He wasn't sure he knew the answer to the question, but he had his suspicions. He knew that Katie had a lot of people she called friends and had a group of about three others who she was close to. He was sure that she told all of these women and occasionally even used them to help her cover up the affair or affairs, although not always, as he discovered during that fateful trip to Las Vegas. Sometimes she got sloppy.

"Katie had a few friends, and I don't know this for a fact, but I suspect she told each of them about her lover or lovers. They did these weekend trips to places like Santa Barbara or Vegas, and I'm sure on some of those trips she either met men there or they went on the trip with her." Mahoney shook his head. He would never tolerate that in his wife, and he was fortunate that she wasn't the type to cheat, or so he thought. As a detective, he was aware that anything was possible and that people often surprise you, but he would bet the farm on Lizzie not running off to Vegas with some rich scumbag. Even when he had first met her all those years ago, she was a down-home girl who believed in being loyal to her husband.

"That must have been hard on you," Mahoney said sounding truly sympathetic. "How did you finally discover that she really was cheating- or didn't you?"

Sanders told him the story about running into one of her friends. "I suspected it for some time," he confessed. "But I was in denial for a long time because I didn't want to lose her. I always felt like I had married up and that maybe one day she would come to her senses and realize what a good catch I was. Katie was – is – a stunning woman. She has that type of beauty that *all* men find attractive. She is sexy as hell, too. We had a great sex life and I thought that would be enough, but she wanted more. Much more. Someone who made a large six-figure income and had the same materialistic values she had. She wanted the expensive handbags from Saks and the $800 shoes. She wanted weekend dinners at Mastro's where she could hobnob with the local rich and famous."

At that moment, Mahoney's cell phone began to ring. It had been so quiet that the sound made both men jump just a little. Mahoney reached into his pocket to pull out the phone. "Mahoney here," he said. A long pause and then "Okay. We'll be there soon."

Sanders waited to hear what the call was about before reacting. He assumed they would be heading out the door to talk to someone about the case.

"That was Jessica Howard at the yoga studio. She wanted us to come by to talk about something she thought might be useful. Let's go now. We can stop by a drive-through and get something to eat along the way. From the tone of her voice, this sounded like it might be good."

Chapter 35

Jessica was waiting for them at the reception desk at the studio. At this time of the day, there were no classes going on, although the manager informed the two detectives that there had been a smaller noon class that had fallen by the wayside after the murder. There was another young woman at reception with blue-black hair that hung to her waist. She had striking blue eyes and a wide nose that somehow made her look even more attractive. She was one of the Pilates instructors whom Jessica thought the detectives should talk to. They had never met her before, but apparently, she had something to say.

"This is Rochelle," said Jess, introducing them to the dark-haired Pilates instructor.

"Hi," said Rochelle, flashing a big smile. "My name is Rochelle Cooper, and I teach here a few days a week. I only teach Pilates," she added as if that was an important tidbit of information. Both men extended their hands.

"Rochelle thinks she might know something that could be of use to you. I know you were asking if we knew whether our victim had been having an affair. Rochelle may be able to help you with that," Jessica gestured to the other woman. She then lowered her head to go back to doing what she had been doing before. Rochelle took over.

"Please, sit down," she said, indicating a small bench just large enough to fit one normal sized person. She was dressed in street clothes, a pair of tight light-colored jeans and a pink V-neck sweater draped over her tall, lean figure. She pushed her long, thick hair away from her face. "Would you like a cup of hot tea?" she asked, going toward the small station where there were herbal teas and a water cooler that required a cup or water bottle to cut back on plastic usage.

"I'm good," said the older detective as he tried to squeeze himself into the small bench. The reception area reminded Mahoney of the way things looked back in the 70s when had been a teen. He realized he probably had been whole lot smaller back then too.

"I'll have some water," said Sanders as he watched her gracefully move toward the tea station. She had a small cup that she used to fill with the cold water. Sanders noticed that she had the graceful body of a ballet dancer.

"So, gentlemen," she said, as she sat down on the floor with her legs crossed yoga style and pulled her abundant hair into a high ponytail. "I understand you are looking for some more information on who Rebekah associated with while she was a student here." Her voice went up at the end of each sentence as if she were asking a question.

"That's right," said Sanders. "Anything you have will be of help to us. We've been trying to figure out if maybe she was involved in a romantic relationship. Maybe someone she met here."

Rochelle inhaled deeply and closed her eyes as if she were in deep thought. Did she know something or was she trying to remember? The men figured this is how people who teach Pilates and yoga do their thinking. It was okay; they had time.

"I confess that initially, she wasn't one of my clients. Her regular instructor, Kim, saw her two, maybe three, times a week. Rebekah was very committed to Pilates, and yoga for that matter." She took a sip of tea from a small paper cup that she had balanced between her legs.

At this point a few people started to walk into the studio. Jessica looked up from the front desk and signed them into the computer. She tried to focus on the business at hand and let Rochelle handle the interview. Sanders watched the manager out of the corner of his eye, noticing how attractive and professional she was. At first, he had been attracted to her slender figure and flawless, well-sculpted face, but now he found her ability to work and concentrate during a difficult time very appealing. He realized that maybe it had been too long since he had been with a woman. He turned his gaze back to Rochelle, trying his best to ignore Jessica.

"One morning," said Rochelle as she opened her eyes wide as if wakening from a deep sleep, "Kim was sick and asked me to teach for her. Between us," she said lowering her voice and shifting her body so that one knee was off the ground and the other tucked behind her, "Kim suffers from insomnia. I had suggested several holistic approaches to this, but I'm not sure she took my advice. So one morning she wasn't up to teaching, so I took over for her. I normally start later in the morning, but I needed the money and I wanted to help her out." She changed the cross of her legs while the two detectives watched, amazed that she could do that so easily.

"And?" asked Mahoney as he stretched his long legs in front of him. The seat was not meant for sitting for any length of time. He was anxious to get to the point of the meeting.

"Well, Rebekah took to me right away," she said with a twinkle in her eye. "So much so that I was worried that she might want to continue with me and drop Kim. That," she said, shaking her head, "is a real no- no. We don't poach clients from each other, but sometimes a client just prefers another teacher, and that can get awkward." After she signed in the last person for the new class being offered, Jessica looked over in the direction of the meeting. The studio was offering a 'try before you buy' class in order to increase the membership, and to give people a chance to see if they preferred yoga or Pilates, or both. She gave Rochelle a critical look. Apparently talking about poaching clients was something they didn't discuss openly.

"As I was saying," Rochelle continued using a quieter voice. "Rebekah and I hit it off. Sometimes clients want to work out hard and they don't want to chat or get to know us at all. In that case, I just push them and focus entirely on the exercise. Then there are those," she added, "who want to share their life stories with you. That day Rebekah was in the mood to tell me her deepest and darkest secrets."

Mahoney cleared his throat and stood up for a moment to stretch out his back. His lower back and right hip were killing him. so he moved around a bit, trying to work out the kinks. Rochelle eyed him as he tried to stretch out his body.

"You should sign up for my beginner Pilates class," she said. "I think it would take care of some of that tightness."

"Maybe," he replied in a tone of voice that revealed it would be unlikely. He wasn't much of an exercise guy other than long walks on Sunday and the occasional session with barbells at the gym.

"I mean it," she said with a flirtatious smile. "I'll make sure to get you one of my cards."

"Tell us about your client's – um – deepest and darkest secrets," asked Sanders, using the same words she used to describe their session. He tried to avoid using sarcasm in his request so she wouldn't take it the wrong way. "Tell us what she told you that day."

"Well, it was more than one day," Rochelle said. "Rebekah seemed to like my sessions, so she changed her times so she could see me instead of Kim. Not for long, mind you, as I told her that it would cause tension if I took her over as a client. So she pretended she needed to change her times for a few weeks, and we found a time that Kim wasn't available, but I was." She lowered her voice as she offered this bit of information. "Like I said, I don't make a habit of poaching clients, but she seemed adamant, so we came up with a plan." She glanced over at the manager, who was busy working at the front desk, to see if she was listening in. It wasn't something Jessica needed to hear. She lowered her voice a notch. "That happens here. Sometimes clients want to change their coach and it can cause some tension within the staff. Trust me, it happens a lot. Anyway," she continued, "Rebekah hinted to me that she was getting into her best shape ever so she could look good for a new man.

195

She mentioned that he was quite a bit younger, fit and extremely handsome. She said that she felt a bit uncomfortable around him due to that middle-aged belly she had and wanted to work hard to get rid of it."

"Did she ever tell you who it was? A name perhaps? More information on where he worked or where he lived?" Mahoney returned to his seat and made his peace with the uncomfortable piece of furniture.

"She never told me any of that. All she told me was that he was younger and hot. She was a lovely woman and looked amazing for her age, but she seemed very proud of herself for finding a younger and good-looking man. Telling me any more than that would be too much information." She said toying with her hair. "When my clients and students open up to me, they usually give me enough information so I know why they want to get into tip-top shape, but the details aren't important. I mean, in the past I've had people go into great detail about what they do in their private time and it can get uncomfortable for me. Rebekah wasn't at all that way. For her it was just a way to get me to push her a little harder."

Sanders glanced over at his partner to see what his reaction was. Did he think that this woman knew more than she was willing to say? Was she afraid to tell them the whole truth? Mahoney's face revealed nothing. He was jotting all this down in his notebook.

"So she never said anything about her alleged affair?" asked Sanders." "Do you have any idea who it could have been?"

Rochelle shook her head. "Honestly, if I knew more, I'd tell you. I didn't tell Jessica about it earlier because I had forgotten. It wasn't like was spent all of our sessions talking about sex."

Mahoney jumped in. "Did she say anything else to you that you think may be of relevance to our investigation?"

The Pilates instructor hesitated. "I don't think so," she said standing up from her pretzel-like position. She then placed her hands on her hips and glanced over at the younger detective. "Whoever it was or, for that matter, still is, she thought he was a good catch. She talked about his hard body and how good he was in bed." Sanders blushed while Mahoney didn't move a muscle. "She wanted to talk about it quite a bit during one of our sessions," Rochelle continued. "but after that she rarely mentioned it. I let it go. It wasn't my place to ask questions. Then," she added. "I stopped seeing her as a client and Kim resumed. It happened rather organically and no one ever said anything more about it."

Two slender young women walked in and walked right up to the instructor despite her being surrounded by law enforcement. They apparently felt no reason whatsoever to feel inhibited. Rochelle lifted her hand signaling for them to stop for a second as she finished up. The two women reluctantly stepped aside and waited across the room. "Those are my clients," she said putting her hand by the side of her mouth and speaking in a whisper. "I do need to stop here and get back to work, but I sincerely hope that I was of some help. "Also," she said turning toward the two men. "I wasn't at the open house the other day so I can't say whether or not she was hanging out with anyone or seemed to be flirting. You may want to ask around to see if anyone else noticed anything. In the meantime, detectives," she extended a beautifully manicured hand, "it was a pleasure meeting you."

The front area was getting busy, so it appeared that the unsolved murder had done little to hurt their business. If anything, Mahoney noticed, it seemed to help. There was an endless flow of lean, muscular bodies coming up the stairs. It was as if nothing had ever happened.

"So, what do you think about that?" asked Sanders quietly so as not to be heard by the people mingling around. They nodded to the manager, who was busy at her desk, informing them they were getting ready to leave. Mahoney stopped for a second to glance back at the reception desk before speaking. "I think our suspect may be closer than we think."

Chapter 36

Mahoney decided to pay yet another visit to Hunter King, now known as husband number two. His trip up to Beverly Hills the day before had left many unanswered questions, but he was starting to get a better feel for who exactly Rebekah King was. She was impulsive, inconsiderate, and strangely, not as materialistic as one would expect. Given her background and her apparent penchant for wealthy men, she didn't follow the path of someone who cared deeply about money. Unlike the women who strolled about Southcoast Plaza carrying shopping bags from exclusive retailers while holding hands with their ancient husbands, she left behind a closet full of designer clothes. Some women would kill to have a successful husband like Keith Goldberg, yet she just ran off for no apparent reason. Was there something the doctor wasn't telling him?

What did Hunter know about Keith Goldberg, and was there any tension between them? Why did Rebekah leave her first husband, and was Hunter privy to any of this information? Early in their marriage, before all the tension, he probably asked about it. What spouse doesn't ask questions about a previous marriage?

He wasn't sure what he thought about Hunter King. Was he the kind of person who would kill his former wife?

You never really knew what anyone was capable of. He remembered a 40-year-old schoolteacher with a stellar reputation who stabbed her husband thirteen times after he told her he wanted a divorce. No one believed that she was capable of speaking her mind, much less committing murder. Her short dark hair and knee length skirts were reminiscent of the way women looked and dressed back in the 1960s. Yet she had snapped, grabbed a sharp kitchen knife, and sliced her husband to bits. People were capable of anything.

Mahoney drove down PCH oblivious to the coastal views and spectacular homes that lined the highway. He took this drive so often that it was becoming old hat. When he saw movies that pictured some old convertible being driven along the coast, it reminded him that he lived in a place where a lot of people would love to be. But when seen time and time again, it lost some if its appeal. Today, however, the ocean however looked unusually calm and the waves sparkled with the sun's yellow rays.

Mahoney was always amazed at the number of luxury cars in their shiny glory on the highway. Mercedes, Jaguars, Ferraris and more. Rarely did he see a plain vanilla Corolla or a Ford sedan. Who were these people and how did they make all this money? The homes facing the highway were perfectly designed mansions with manicured lawns and elaborate patios. The larger mansions facing away from the busy Pacific Coast highway boasted beautiful ocean views that sold for as much as $20 million during heady economic times. Most of these homes were owned by successful business owners and old-moneyed families that came here from a variety of states and countries. It was the kind of wealth that Mahoney could never imagine. To him, being rich enough meant being able to pay the bills each month and schedule a week-long vacation with his wife. He didn't need the fancy car and the 3500 square foot house. He was glad he married a woman who didn't need all the trappings either. She was perfectly happy with the life she had. Or was she? Was she like so many other women who desired a man who could take financial care of them, allowing them the option to stop work at any time? He was certain that Lizzie loved her job, despite the long hours and the stress of working under so much pressure. Maybe if he had been more successful, she could work fewer hours or take on a job that required little or no stress. He never asked her how she felt about her job and whether it was something she really wanted to do. No-nonsense Lizzie with her sensible clothes and low-maintenance appearance rarely complained. He thought she was the most beautiful woman in the world, and even though there were hundreds, if not thousands, of beautiful women in Orange County, no one could hold a candle to her.

Mahoney pulled up to the King house, which was hidden behind tall trees. Two Mexican gardeners were carrying large plastic garbage bags to their truck while another was clipping the bushes. Despite the grandeur of the houses in this area, they were all squeezed in close together. Unlike homes in more rural areas, there was no space between them. Each backyard had a swimming pool, deck, and outdoor grill. He wondered if these wealthy families gathered around the BBQ on Sunday afternoons with hamburgers and hot dogs for large family cookouts like they did in the Midwest or Southeast. Perhaps they were mostly for show giving the impression that the *perfect* American family lived inside. When one neighbor had the top-of-the-line backyard, the others would quickly follow. Being rich, thought the detective, was not always that much fun. The whole idea of keeping up with the Joneses put a sour taste in his mouth. It was a lose-lose battle and he wanted no part of it.

As he pulled up in front of the house, he could see that Hunter King's black Mercedes was parked in front. He imagined that the girlfriend's car was parked in the garage along with another car or two. Perhaps they had just returned from an errand. He walked up the path to the large red door. He rang the bell and waited. He could hear a small dog barking inside and someone calling that she would be right down. He waited a few more seconds before the door was opened by the young girlfriend dressed in tight navy yoga pants and a skimpy sports bra. Her long brown hair was piled high on her head in the ubiquitous messy bun and her face was make-up free. She was still stunning, even without the help of make-up.

"Hi," she said in a voice that sounded like she was 12 years old. "Are you here to speak with Hunter?" she asked, striking a sexy pose that probably would turn on most straight men.

"Yes. Is he here?" Mahoney took two steps back from the young woman. He didn't want to get too close.

"Hey Huntie," she called. "Someone is here to see you," She turned back to the detective and gestured for him to come inside. "He's just getting out of the shower," she said pointing to the large white sofa where they had conducted their last interview. There was a large wide screen TV, and an exercise video was playing. Someone who looked a lot like Hunter's girlfriend was demonstrating a series of exercises with weights and bands. "He'll be right down," she said and went right back to exercising. Mahoney crossed his legs and pulled out his notes.

"Is that your sister?" asked Mahoney, as he was now convinced that the woman demonstrating the exercises looked exactly like her.

"Who?" She asked lifting a barbell over her head and bringing it down to her shoulders. "Her?"

"She looks a lot like you. You could be twins."

"Eww," she said putting the weight down. "She's at least five years older than me and a good ten pounds heavier." She patted her flat stomach. "I work really hard to have this," she added sounding annoyed with the detective. She lifted the weights and kept moving.

"I'm sorry," he said. He truly was sorry he even brought it up.

She shrugged and continued doing exactly what the woman on the screen was doing. A few seconds later, Mahoney could hear someone coming down the long spiral staircase. There was Hunter King wearing a long blue bathrobe, his thick hair still wet. He carried a bath towel in his hand and was running it over his head as he descended the staircase.

"Detective Mahoney, right?" he said. "Good to see you again." The detective knew for certain that he wasn't glad to see him again at all.

"Mr. King. Good to see you too. Sorry to disturb your shower."

"Not at all. Not at all," he said tossing the towel on a chair. "What can I do for you on this lovely Tuesday morning? It is Tuesday isn't it?" he said gesturing to the large open window that faced the swimming pool. His girlfriend continued to move with the older, heavier exercise instructor until Hunter gave her a look. She turned off the TV, picked up her weights and walked out without saying a word.

Hunter shook his head as his pretty mistress stomped up the stairs. By her demeanor, she was not ready to end her exercise session.

"Not the sharpest tool in the shed," he commented as he watched her walk up the stairs. "She's a beauty, that's for sure, but you can't have everything can you? Can I get you something to drink, Detective? I have sparkling water, fresh squeezed orange juice and this amazing lemonade we get at Gelson's that tastes like you made it yourself."

"No, thank you. I'm fine," said the detective as he leaned forward in his seat. He felt funny talking to this tall, handsome man who was prancing around in a bathrobe. It was as if Mahoney was at the Playboy mansion and interviewing Hugh himself. He wished King would go upstairs and change into something – anything – but he was going to have to conduct the interview as is.

"Mr. King. Can you tell me what you know…?"

"Please," Hunter said, crossing his long legs. "Call me Hunter. Amelia," he called out to the kitchen. "Please bring me two glasses of that lemonade we bought the other day. No ice, please. Sorry, please, go on. You were saying?"

"I was going to ask you about Dr. Keith Goldberg, Rebekah's first husband. Can you tell me anything about their relationship?"

Hunter King's face changed suddenly. Mahoney had struck a chord. "Dr. Goldberg. Good plastic surgeon. Did you know he sees all the top movie stars and even had the wife of a sultan escorted in for a $100,000 face lift?" Despite his words, the look on his face revealed that he didn't appreciate hearing the name of his ex-wife's ex-husband.

"That's great, but that's not the information I am looking for."

"No. Of course not. Actually, I know very little about her ex-husband.' Amelia had brought in two glasses of lemonade and Hunter picked up his glass to take a sip. "I asked her about him early in the marriage. I was curious as to why their marriage dissolved so quickly. I told her about my earlier marriages with the hope that we wouldn't make the same mistakes twice. She wasn't as willing to share with me."

"What did she tell you? There must have been something?"

"I knew about Boston and how she left one night with just a few suitcases. She also suggested that he was a workaholic," he laughed. "Aren't we all, though? I mean the man rakes in well over a million a year and is listed as one of the top plastic surgeons in the world and she runs off to Boston with two suitcases? I should have seen that as a red flag from the get-go." Mahoney didn't respond. He believed that Hunter King knew more than he was saying.

"When she told me about her first husband," he continued with his legs crossed and his bathrobe opened slightly, making Mahoney feel even more uncomfortable, "I envisioned a Jewish doctor who had a thing for blonde, blue-eyed girls. A short fellow with a huge chip on his shoulder. But further research showed that he was a nice-looking guy and really good at what he did." He cleared his throat. "Despite all that, I guess he wasn't able to satisfy her and that's why she left," He smiled. *Arrogant prick* thought Mahoney.

Mahoney put down the pen and took a deep breath before continuing. He felt if Hunter King said anything else even remotely narcissistic he would punch him squarely in the nose. "Mr. King," he said refusing to use his first name. "Can you tell me anything that can help me understand why she left her first husband so abruptly?"

I really don't know much, detective. If I did, I would tell you." He stood up, pulling the belt on his robe tighter before sitting back down. "Is Dr. Goldberg a suspect?" He sounded almost giddy when he asked the question.

"Right now everyone is a suspect," Mahoney replied.

"Well, if you want to know if her first husband had a motive, I would say yes. I think the divorce was a big slap in the face to him, and I don't think he believed the divorce settlement was fair. He never really got over her and the way she stormed out. An ego thing, I guess."

"One more question before I leave," said Mahoney. "Do you think Rebekah was having an affair?"

Hunter King laughed. "Maybe. I mean anything is possible, but the young men simply were not interested in her. Look, Rebekah at one time was a sexy woman. She was never a beauty the way Logan is. Don't get me wrong. Rebekah was sexy once upon a time, but she got old and let herself go." He shook his head. "She had the means to keep herself attractive, but she didn't bother. She seemed to think a bit too highly of herself. Fake confidence is what I call it."

Hunter King curled his legs underneath him and his bathrobe opened up just a little, exposing his upper legs. Mahoney turned away to avoid seeing more than he cared to. All this talk about Rebekah letting herself go was coming from King's own bruised ego. From what Mahoney could gather, she had left him instead of the other way around.

At that point, Logan came prancing down the stairs wearing a summer dress with spaghetti straps and a V-neck. She was not wearing a bra, and her large breasts bounced as she bounded down the stairs. King smiled, showing a sense of pride and ownership in the beautiful young girl bouncing down the stairs. Even the detective couldn't take his eyes off her. King noticed him eyeing her and he smiled knowingly. "'She's hot," he said with a sense of pride. "She is eminently fuckable. Rebekah was not."

"I'm leaving for a bit," said Logan as she put on a pair of black strappy sandals and grabbed a set of car keys from the side table. "I'll be back in a little while," she said.

"Have fun," said Hunter as she left. "Be home for lunch."

"As I was saying," repeated Mahoney, checking his watch for the time. He was hoping for a short meeting this time. He had lunch plans with Lizzie this afternoon and he had a few things he needed to do around the house. Weekends were the only time he could do a little fixing up in their 39-year-old house, but this wasn't a 9 to 5 job, and he would stay as long as he needed to. "One of her Pilates teachers thinks she may have been having an affair and it wasn't the first one. We need to explore all possibilities here, and a former lover is always going to be a prime suspect."

Hunter King waved his hand in disbelief. He stood up and pulled the bathrobe tighter across his body as if just remembering that he wasn't yet dressed. "If she had any romance in her life, it's something recent and not anything that happened during our marriage. She was always loyal to me, even up to the bitter end." He started to walk towards the kitchen with his back turned to the detective. He stopped just short of the large designer kitchen and turned around his hands on his hips. "She was loyal, but I was not. As a matter of fact, I wouldn't have minded at all if she had taken on a young lover or two, as it would have made it easier on me. So any romantic interests she has, or should I say had, in young men is relatively new. I am actually glad she enjoyed herself during her final years. Nothing like a good sex life to enrich your life."

Mahoney nodded but said nothing. He couldn't believe how arrogant this guy was. To even suggest that his wife couldn't attract a lover on the side was egotistical. To claim that he wished she had was obscene.

"Is there anything else you need from me?" Hunter King asked trying to sound as cooperative as possible. "I do have to get dressed and get going here, so if there isn't anything else, I should get moving." Mahoney closed his notebook and stood up. "No, that's all I need for now. If you think of anything that could be helpful, you know how to reach me."

"Thank you, Detective Mahoney. If you don't mind could you let yourself out. I'm in a bit of a rush."

Mahoney walked to the door, taking one last glance at the exquisitely designed house. No detail was left out. A model home where plastic people really didn't do much living. All along this small tree-lined street half a mile from the beach, these five- to ten-million-dollar homes were having work done. New windows, interior remodeling, painting and new landscaping. White vans were as common here as new Maserati.

As he walked down the elegantly maintained pathway with its assortment of orange, pink and yellow flowers, towards his car, he thought about the interview with Hunter King. King was not being completely honest. Mahoney knew that right away from his body language and his rush to end the interview. Mahoney had been in the business long enough to recognize a liar when he met one, and this fellow was lying. But why? Why would he not admit that his ex-wife had been having an affair or a series of affairs? He was cheating, too. He didn't seem like the jealous type, although you never really know. Men didn't usually like the idea of their wives sleeping around, even if they were doing the same. What was good for the goose wasn't always good for the gander. Mahoney got it. If Lizzie so much as kissed a guy on the cheek, he'd fly into a jealous range. An affair? He was convinced he'd go postal. Yet it was different for a man. Mahoney never cheated nor would he ever, but if he did it would be meaningless. He could sleep with a woman and forget her completely the next day. It wasn't the same for women. They tended to fall in love very quickly. To women, affairs had a strong emotional component. Was that what happened with this couple? Did the randy ex-husband think he could handle his wife's cheating and then, one day, finally fly off the handle and kill her?

Mahoney got into his car and put the keys in the ignition but stayed put. Several people glanced his way, thinking he must be the help, otherwise he would be driving a nicer car. They nodded at him and moved on. It was the type of neighborhood that expected outsiders to come in, do some work on the house or garden and then leave before sunset. They didn't want you to stay for too long. He scratched his head, trying to make sense of what Hunter King had said. Did Rebekah cheat on him during the marriage, making it impossible to stay with her? Did she take him to the cleaners with the divorce settlement, and had she been asking for more? It didn't seem that way, but it wasn't impossible. There were a lot of maybes here, and a few suspects, but no one stood out as the one who murdered Rebekah King.

Chapter 37

Nearly the entire staff of Newport Yoga and Pilates fit into the smaller of the two classrooms for the meeting. The female teachers all looked beautiful with their freshly washed hair and figure-hugging clothes.

Jessica had delivered on her promise and brought in some freshly baked croissants and some vegan muffins from the hipster bakery across the street. Most everyone was there except Declan Stevens who, as always, would arrive late and another teacher who was off to India on her annual retreat.

"Okay everyone. Thank you so much for coming this morning. I know you're all busy with classes and family, but this is important, and we need to close this case as soon as possible so we can get back to business as usual. I know some of you had more interaction with the deceased while others of you have absolutely no idea who she was." The manager looked around the room and could see a few of her staff fidgeting, either because they knew something, or they wanted to be somewhere else. "There are two detectives working on this case, and they have been working around the clock to solve it. There is only so much I can do by myself, so I need your help. We're going to go around the room here and everyone please tell me what you know."

She shifted her weight uncomfortably on the green and yellow yoga mat. She used to feel limber and could sit for hours in any pose, but the stress of the investigation was causing her muscles to tighten up more than usual. This was unacceptable, she thought to herself. Working at a yoga studio was supposed to make one more limber and pain-free, not less. She made a mental note to schedule a massage sometime over the weekend. "If you don't know what I am talking about or who I am talking about, just say so. No need to elaborate." At that moment, Declan Stevens walked in carrying a large backpack. He unrolled his yoga mat next to an older yoga teacher and sat down next to her as quietly as possible.

Jessica eyed the yoga teacher and then continued to ask each teacher to share what they knew. "I didn't even know she existed," said one curly haired teacher. "Now that's *all* we talk about." Another admitted to having her in a class or two but knew very little about her. "She moved well enough for an older lady, but other than that I can't say much. She never complained, so yeah, all in all she was a good student. Why anyone would want her dead Is beyond me." The Pilates teachers who knew her more intimately as a client had more to say. There was nothing that they hadn't already told Jessica and the detectives. Declan was the last to speak. He shifted uncomfortably on his thick black yoga mat and started to speak. "I knew her a little," he said, his voice sounding a bit tired and strained. "She was nice. Very nice and a good student of yoga. She was always in a cheerful mood and glad to be here." He looked around the circle, and then added. "Not like so many other students who come here to bitch and complain about one thing or another." Most of the other teachers nodded in agreement. The bitchy student was someone they all had to deal with and no one liked it.

"Did you socialize with her at all?" asked Jessica in a tone of voice that didn't convey suspicion or criticism.

"I had coffee with her once," he said scratching his head. "No. Make that twice. We had coffee together twice." He added scratching his head.

"Have you brought this to the attention of the detectives on the case? I think they need to know every single detail about our interaction with the victim. If you haven't already, you need to do this soon." She added firmly. Declan nodded.

"We need to wrap this case up very soon," she continued. "The future of this studio depends on this. I don't care how full your classes are, or how many people you have booked for Pilates sessions, no one is going to sign up if this case goes unresolved for much longer. Who wants to work out where a murder took place and the killer is still at large? Doesn't make for a good marketing plan, does it?" She was getting angry and wanted to make a point. Most of the teachers had no idea how serious this was.

Declan raised his hand like a child in elementary school trying to please the teacher. "She had been married twice. Once to a man here and the other to a doctor up in LA. Not sure if that helps at all, but I thought I'd bring it up."

"Yes. I think the detectives mentioned that to me. There are two ex-husbands and two suspects but no one has yet to be convicted." Jessica looked around. "Anything else we should know?" There was a lot of mumbling, but no one spoke up. "Well if you know of anything at all, please let me know sooner rather than later." With that she ended the meeting and everyone either stayed put to chat with the person next to them or they got up to leave. "Hold it a second," she said to Declan, who was carefully rolling up his yoga mat. "I need to ask you something."

"Sure. What can I do for you?" Jessica was aware of the charm this teacher had on women, but she didn't find him all that appealing. There was no shortage of good-looking men in Southern California and there was something just a bit too perfect about him. He wasn't her type at all.

Jessica stood up and brushed some crumbs off her shirt – remains from part of an apple pastry that she ate during the meeting. "Tell me more about your coffee meeting with Rebekah. I'm just curious if she spoke to you about anything that might give us some clues." He stretched his limber body like a cat waking up from a nap. Jessica waited for him to respond.

"It wasn't much of anything. I often have coffee with my students. Sometimes a whole group of us head over to Kean's Coffee and shoot the breeze between classes. She was just a nice lady who liked yoga. Nothing less, nothing more."

"Did she talk about her exes with you?"

"No. The topic never came up. She wasn't wearing a wedding ring, so I assumed she was between husbands. Not that unusual among my female students."

"So how did you know about the two ex-husbands. Is that something that normally comes up in conversation?" She realized that she was starting to sound critical and needed to tone it down. "I mean maybe it does. I guess women like to talk to their teachers don't they?"

"Some do and some don't", Declan replied. "I think I asked her once if she was married and she said she had been twice. She told me a little something about the doctor husband in LA because I asked her where she lived when she was there." He shrugged.

Jessica wasn't convinced that Declan was being entirely transparent with her, but she left it at that. If there was more to the relationship between the two of them, it would come out eventually. She made a mental note to call one of the detectives to let them know. She thanked Declan for staying after the meeting.

As she left the building to head home, she decided to call Martin Sanders to let him know what she thought about the meeting. She could have called the more senior detective, but she looked forward to an excuse to talk to Detective Sanders. She realized that she was starting to think about him a little more than she should.

Chapter 38

Jessica was in her car driving home when Detective Sanders returned her call. She pulled into the parking lot of Ralph's so she could focus on the call. She felt butterflies in her stomach upon hearing his voice.

"Jessica," said the detective, sounding relieved he had reached her. "I got a message that you called." Jessica slid her phone into the holder and put him on speaker.

"Thanks for calling me back." She wondered if her voice gave away how nervous she felt. Snap out of it, she told herself. This is so childish. "So, we had our staff meeting not long ago and we went around the room and everyone revealed what they knew about Rebekah."

The detective nodded on the other end, and then realizing she couldn't hear the sound of his nodding said, "Okay. Go on."

"Well, everyone said pretty much what we already know, and some people had no idea who she was. However..." she paused.

"Yes, go on," Sanders said, starting to feel a bit of a tingling deep in his belly, which he tried to ignore.

"However," she repeated not missing a beat. "One of our yoga teachers, Declan Stevens, mentioned that he had coffee with her a few times." Sander's ears perked up upon hearing this. "I tried to get him to say more, but he said it was just coffee and yoga talk. I know that he often meets with the women at the studio to talk about yoga, other teachers, other studios etc., but I don't think he does much more than that. He's been known to date a lot of aspiring actresses and models, so I doubt he feels the need to chase our female clientele," she said.

"So they met for coffee a few times, but that was it. Are you sure it was just a few times?" Sanders pressed her. Jessica bit her lip. She wasn't sure. Declan had an air about him that was hard to read, and she was usually good at reading people. He was very sure of himself, even though his acting career never really took off. He got plenty of admiration from his students, and that was what he craved. It made up for his failed attempt at celebrity.

"I don't know. I'm not sure if I believe him. I believe he had coffee with her, but I'm not sure that was the extent of it. He's very much a ladies' man. Men like him too, but I think he's straight. Maybe bi, but he seems to prefer women." Sanders let that sink in. He remembered seeing Declan Stevens on one occasion and he noticed that he was a very attractive man in his 30s. He understood why women would be attracted to him. He had an air of cockiness that he tried to pass off as confidence; Sanders could spot that in a man a mile away. Because Stevens was a teacher of a very physical and sensual form of exercise, women had even more reason to fall for him. Katie would have probably slept with him a few times, but she wouldn't want anything more from him. She tended to gravitate toward men with substantial bank accounts.

"Does he have a reputation with the women? Does he sleep around? You might want to find out. Has he ever hit on *you*?" Sanders secretly hoped that hadn't been the case.

"No," she laughed. "I'm not his type. He tends to prefer older women with nice bodies who absolutely adore him." Sanders started to say that she, too, had a nice body but caught himself just in time. "He's an okay guy, however," she continued to say. "And a very good teacher. He has a large following, and in this business, a following is everything."

"Well, sounds to me like it may be worth looking into. Let me give Mahoney a call and see what we can do. It's a long shot, but worth meeting with him." She agreed and they said their good-byes. When she hung up the phone and restarted the car, she suddenly felt energized. She realized she was developing a little crush on the detective and for the first time in a long time, she was feeling really good.

Chapter 39

Detective Martin Sanders thought about his recent phone conversation with the studio manager. He was concerned about what she told him. He barely remembered Declan Stevens from the time they met right after the body was discovered, but he remembered a youngish, good-looking man who seemed genuinely concerned about what had happened to Rebekah King. He felt it was time to pay the yoga teacher a visit. He had all the information he needed, so Sanders decided to show up unannounced. Worst case scenario, he wouldn't be there, and Sanders would have to call him to schedule a better time. He had already checked the on-line scheduling app to see when Stevens taught yoga so he knew exactly when not to go.

He arrived at Stevens' yellow and green bungalow tucked behind a bigger stone house on a quiet tree-lined street in Costa Mesa. He had always wanted to buy a house in this neighborhood, but a 1500 square- foot fixer-upper with a decent yard was well over his budget. It had become a trendy area among the millennials who worked high income jobs or those who were blessed with wealthy parents and healthy trust funds. Real estate had been such a good investment in Southern California that some parents invested in homes for their children and had them pay rent in return. Sanders figured that this Stevens fellow probably came from money. It wasn't likely that yoga teachers, successful or otherwise, would qualify for such a large mortgage. Then again, Stevens might just be renting.

Sanders decided he had waited long enough and got out of the car, walking toward the bungalow that was set back from the street behind a larger two-story home. A middle-aged woman wearing a scarf around her head and heavy-duty gardening gloves was working in front of the larger house. She eyed the detective suspiciously as he walked to the bungalow. He nodded at her and she went back to her gardening without saying a word. He wondered if this woman owned the smaller house and rented it out. It would explain how Declan could afford to live in this affluent area.

He gave three slow knocks on the front door. He waited a few seconds before starting to knock again, when he heard someone call from the back of the house. "Coming." He waited patiently, looking at the well-kept potted plants along the front of the house. An effort had been made to keep the grounds looking nice. A few tall potted succulents in various shades of green, yellow and orange lined the entry way. Katie could never maintain a garden like this one. She didn't have the patience.

Declan opened the door; he was dressed in a colorful Tommy Bahama-style Hawaiian shirt and a pair of loose-fitting beige shorts. The detective noticed his muscular and tanned legs and was impressed that yoga could produce such good muscle tone. Dressed the way he was and with the great tan, Sanders figured that Declan was also a surfer.

"Come on in," he said gesturing for Sanders to come inside. They entered a small living area that was neat and comfortable. However, there was only one very small sofa and not a single chair.

"May I sit?" Sanders asked, looking around at the scarcity of furniture in the room. It looked like something out of a 1960s commune, with long strands of beads used as dividers between the main living area and what appeared to be a small kitchen. There was a thick black yoga mat in the corner and a stick of incense burning inside a Buddha-like incense holder. The room smelled of lemon and spice. He looked around to see two yellow candles burning on a coffee table. There was also a stick of incense burning in a holder on a bookshelf. Declan seemed confused at the question then realized that the detective was probably not in the habit of sitting crossed legged on the floor. He nodded and rushed into the attached room to get a folding chair. He set it up so the detective could sit down comfortably. "I'm sorry," he said grabbing a small purple pillow from the floor. "I normally sit on the floor, so I don't use chairs that much." He placed the small cushion on the chair. "Here you go," he said gesturing to the guest. "I'll just sit over here," he said, pointing to the mini sofa.

The detective sat down on the chair and pulled out his notepad and pen. "Can I get you some tea?" Declan remained standing. Sanders noticed that he was even better looking than he had originally thought. Sanders realized that someone with this physique would be able to attract a lot of female students. He wondered if he would have been his ex-wife's type. Probably not, as she tended to focus more on the size of the bank account and less on the size of the biceps "I have a few flavors if you'd like." The detective shook his head. He wouldn't have minded a cup of hot coffee, but he didn't want to waste the time.

"I'm good. I had coffee before getting here." He readjusted his long legs, trying to make himself comfortable. "Now, this is what I need to discuss with you, Mr. Stevens." For some reason he didn't want to use the name 'Declan' because it sounded so affected and he didn't know what else to call him. "I understand," he continued glancing down at his notes "that you spent some time with the victim. It looks like you had coffee with her a few times after class." He started to say something else but thought better of it.

"Yes. That's true. We had coffee a couple of times over at that coffee shop near the studio." A long sharp whistling noise came from the kitchen. "Excuse me while I get the kettle off the stove and make some tea." He walked through the hanging beads into the kitchen. Sanders waited for him to return.

He came back carrying a mug of hot tea. He seemed very relaxed, despite the presence of a detective in his living room. He certainly didn't seem the slightest bit nervous about being questioned.

"We spoke sometimes after class," he said taking a sip of tea from his cup. "Not after every class, but sometimes. Why? Do you find that to be unusual?"

"Unusual? Yes, a bit. I would think that the studio would frown on relationships between teachers and students. Isn't that the case?" Declan shrugged and took another sip of tea. He didn't seem overly concerned with rules.

"We have a policy where socializing with clients isn't encouraged, but many of the teachers end up sooner or later socializing with their students. Yoga can be very inclusive that way." Sanders raised his eyebrows, not knowing exactly what that meant, but he let it go. "Some of my students are anxious to get home to their families," continued Declan. "Others have hot dates and they squeeze their daily yoga in before meeting up at some trendy new bar. Then there is – was -- Rebekah. She always had time. She was rarely in a rush and usually had time to chat after class. She seemed very interested in yoga. At least it seemed that way." There was no defensiveness in his voice. He seemed very comfortable with the relationship they had. Sanders wondered if it was really the yoga she was interested in, but he kept that to himself. "Once or twice we went out for a cup of coffee or a juice after class, but not often." He shrugged. "I'm aware of how that looks," he said reading the detective's thoughts. "Besides, there was a bit of an age difference, and it would have been awkward." The detective nodded. He wasn't taking notes. "You see, I think she had misconceptions of where this was going. I thought of her as a friend. A student I could meet with and talk about yoga or the environment. But she had other ideas. She was falling for me." He shook his head and for a second looked dejected. Sanders wondered if maybe this young yoga teacher felt bad about giving his student the wrong impression. Could he be feeling guilty?

"So there was no romantic involvement then?" Sanders asked raising his eyebrows.

"Oh, no. Not at all. Like I said, I strongly suspect that she wanted more from me than I was willing to give, and that became strange. I had to be careful not to cause her to leave the studio because that could reflect poorly on me." Sanders nodded. He understood the policy that the studio had discouraging teachers from getting romantically involved with students. He also understood that sometimes older women were reluctant to make the moves on much younger men, mostly due to fear of rejection. Yet in Rebekah's case, she wasn't used to rejection. In everything he had learned about her, she wasn't the least bit shy. Facing rejection from someone she desired must have been hard on her. On the other hand, Stevens could also be lying. If she had become a stalker of sorts and threatened him in any way, that would give him motive.

"Is there anything else you could tell me about Rebekah King that might help us in the investigation?"

Declan Stevens leaned back thinking it over. He took a few seconds to answer. "She was a nice enough person, but she had a lot of issues." He said looking down at his feet.

"Issues? Can you elaborate?" Sanders was pleased that it was easy enough to get him to speak openly and honestly.

"She wasn't happy. Her last marriage ended badly, and she seemed determined to find another rich man to take care of her. At her age and with the competition here in Southern California, she wasn't having much luck. I listened to her complain about the shortage of straight men in the area, but it started to get old. I found excuses not to meet with her after class."

"I see," said Sanders. He believed Stevens, as the story rang true to life. The victim was obviously a very unhappy and lonely woman who had fallen for her yoga teacher.

Sadly, he hadn't felt the same way about her. Yet given what Sanders already knew about Rebekah, she didn't seem like the type to latch on to someone like that. Had she changed? Had she been feeling as desperate as Declan had made her out to be?

Sanders stood up and put the notepad back in his jacket pocket. "I think that's all I need," he said, heading towards the front door. "Oh, and I forgot to ask. Did she ever say anything about her first husband? He was an LA surgeon. I think they got divorced years ago."

"As a matter of fact, if I remember correctly, she said that she and her ex from LA had dinner that night. The night of our open house that is. Yeah, she told me that they met at some chic Mexican place in Costa Mesa and that the dinner didn't go all that well."

Sanders thought that through. The very same night that she was murdered, she met her first ex-husband at a local restaurant, argued with him about something, and then went on to the yoga studio for a party. This was the first he heard about the dinner with the ex, and the timing was noteworthy.

"Can you tell me what you mean by it not going well? Did she share any of this information with you at the party? Did they argue? Did they kiss and make up?" Sanders pressed for more information.

The yoga teacher shook his head. "No. She didn't go into a lot of detail. You have to understand that the party was – well – very loud. Besides, at that point I had distanced myself from her and I wasn't interested in any long conversations. She just came over to me while I was talking to someone else and mentioned that she had dinner with her ex and when I asked her how it went she made a face."

Sanders wondered about the meeting with the first ex-husband. He needed to get on the phone with his partner as soon as possible. The fact they met so close to the time she was murdered was something that had to be looked into.

The detective checked his watch and thanked the young man for his time. The teacher thanked him for stopping by and opened the door for him. "Let me know if I can help you with anything else," he said, leaning against the door. Sanders nodded and walked down the pathway to his car. The woman was still out there pulling weeds and discarding them in a large green bin. This time she smiled as he walked by. As he reached his car and opened the door, he felt a sense of accomplishment and was sure he was one step closer to finding who killed Rebekah King. He still didn't know who had murdered her, but he felt like he was narrowing down the suspects. Sanders felt certain that Declan Stevens knew more than he was willing to reveal. Then there was the first ex-husband who had lied to Mahoney about his contact with Rebekah. Maybe it was time to revisit the husband number 1 and find out what happened on that fateful night.

Chapter 40

Sanders called his partner on his way back to the station but his call went directly to voicemail. "Mahoney call me as soon as possible. Got something to tell you."

The meeting with Declan Stevens had been more informative than he had expected. Sanders wasn't sure what he had initially expected from the yoga teacher, but it wasn't much. Sanders found him to be more amenable and less arrogant than he originally thought. He also provided some good information. Could it be possible that Rebekah was not the femme fatale that Angela painted her out to be? Could she have been an angry and vindictive person, which resulted in her brutal murder? He was starting to see things differently.

As he exited onto the freeway his cell phone buzzed. He picked up right away.

"Where the hell have you been Mahoney?" He shouted into the phone. "I've been trying to reach you."

"I didn't realize I had to be available to you 24/7," said Mahoney half kidding. "If you must know, I've been very busy working on this murder case. I hope you have some valuable information for me, Sanders." Sanders smiled. He finally had something to give the cranky old man.

"I do have something for you," Sanders said as he swerved to miss a motorcycle that was zigzagging between lanes. He hit his horn and the motorcyclist flipped him the bird. "Asshole," he said out loud.

"You calling me an asshole?" Mahoney asked indignantly.

"Not you, asshole," he said laughing. "I just went to east side Costa Mesa to meet with that Declan Stevens fellow following up on a lead I got from the studio. I was told that he met with Rebekah frequently after class. I guess they had a few post-yoga coffee dates that didn't go unnoticed by some of the other teachers." Sanders was pleased to have been the one to discover this.

"Hmm," replied Mahoney, sounding distracted and somewhat unimpressed. "Where are you now? Close enough to be here in less than fifteen minutes?"

"I could be there in ten," Sanders lied. It would be at least fifteen minutes with traffic the way it was. Mahoney could wait. "Oh," he said nonchalantly before he hung up. "Did you know that Rebekah had dinner with her first ex-husband, you know, the surgeon guy from LA, the very same night she was murdered?" He knew that this bit of information would impress the older detective.

There was a pause on the other end of the line. *Bingo!* thought Sanders. He got his partner's attention. A real victory. He also knew that Mahoney would downplay his coup, but he didn't care. "When I met with the doctor husband, he didn't mention that he had dinner with his ex that night. I wonder why that is? For whatever reason, he didn't want me to know."

Sanders was a bit surprised by the response. Mahoney was actually right. If Dr. Goldberg had been up to no good that evening, he wouldn't mention the dinner. If they discovered this bit of information later on, as they were sure to do, then he could just say that it was a casual dinner, and nothing happened. "I gotta go. I'll be in my office when you get here. Drive faster. I got somewhere to be this evening," Mahoney said before hanging up.

Chapter 41

Sanders arrived at the station in a record seventeen minutes. He managed to get through each and every light along the way and to maintain a steady speed of at least 10 miles over the speed limit. Being a cop had its advantages. When he finally arrived at the precinct he found Mahoney on the phone with his long legs propped up on the desk. Mahoney was deep in conversation but motioned for him to come in and take a seat. "Okay. I'll see you later this evening. Order me a diet coke if I'm running late," Mahoney said to whomever he was talking to on the phone. "Love you too," he said and hung up. "That was Lizzie," he said focusing his attention on his partner. "We have a dinner date tonight at this Greek restaurant she loves." He glanced at his watch. "I need to be out of here in a half hour. Promised the wife I wouldn't be late. So tell me what you found out today."

Sanders pulled the notebook from his jacket pocket and looked through his notes. He knew everything that had happened during the meeting, but he needed to convince Mahoney that what he learned today was true. "Well, it seemed that Rebekah had a thing for Declan Stevens. That is," he said looking up from his notes, "according to him. Apparently a lot of the female students develop crushes on yoga teachers, especially good-looking ones like him, and I guess he doesn't discourage it." Mahoney shrugged. What else is new? he thought. Women and men who work together or are in class together develop crushes all the time. That wasn't anything new. "According to Mr. Stevens, our victim seemed lonely and needy," Sanders continued, trying to present the material in the best light possible. Sanders knew that his partner could be stubborn and didn't like it when someone else discovered something meaningful to the case. He wanted to be able to take credit for everything related to the case. "The Rebekah King he described doesn't sound like the same woman her *best friend* described to us. In other words," he added leaning forward his eyes shining, "the middle-aged femme fatale who seemed irresistible to men of all shapes, sizes and ages had found the one man who wasn't into her." Mahoney stared straight ahead but said nothing. The pause seemed to last an eternity and Sanders fidgeted as he waited for a reply.

"So," said Mahoney finally. "whaddya think? Do you believe that the yoga teacher gave her the brush-off after a torrid affair that didn't last as long as she had hoped it would? You know what they say: Hell hath no fury as a woman scorned or something like that," he said shaking his head. "Sounds like a woman scorned to me."

"Except she was the one who was killed, not him." Mahoney gave him a look that stopped Sanders from saying more. "I know that. Maybe she had the goods on him and was going to snitch. Maybe they got into a fight and she lost. I mean who knows. It's all very possible."

"Yeah, but Declan wasn't married, and according to Angela Demarco, the supposed best friend, she liked to sleep with younger men and then dump them. Why would she change all of a sudden and fall deeply in lust with someone she knew she couldn't have? Doesn't sound like her. Of course everything about this woman is one big mystery."

"I don't know why, but it happens. Middle-aged woman sleeps around, decides she really likes this yoga teacher and then gets all bent out of shape when he dumps her." Mahoney furrowed his eyebrows. "If she wanted the alleged affair to keep going and he was ready to move on, she may have threatened him with something."

"With what? He didn't have any money that we know of, and the worst that could happen is he could have lost his job. Not a big deal for a good-looking guy like Declan. Think about it, Sanders. This would give her a motive to strangle the guy, not the other way around, Middle aged woman seduces younger men; decides she likes the hot yoga teacher and then strangles him with a shoelace when he tells her that she's too old for him." The detective placed his hands on his hips and shook his head. "Nope. This doesn't make any sense. At this point I am almost ready to rule this guy out. If anything, he is nursing a broken heart at this time and simply doesn't want us to know," Sanders said, raising his voice just enough to express the frustration he felt. Mahoney glanced at his watch and held up five fingers "That's all I got. So what else did you learn from your visit with the sexy yoga guru?"

Sanders leaned against the wall and looked very proud of himself. "Turns out that on the night of the event, ex-husband number one paid his ex-wife a visit, and they had dinner right before she made an appearance at the studio. Apparently it didn't go so well." Mahoney raised his eyebrows and looked up from his desk. "I think it might be best if you go visit the LA doctor alone. He might not like the two of us ganging up on him while he gets ready to fix someone's nose. Sanders put his hand on the doorknob and began to turn it. "I've got a few things to do tomorrow, so I suggest you take a trip up to Beverly Hills without me," Sanders said and then walked out the door.

Chapter 42

Mahoney stared at the door of his office for a full minute before he decided he needed to do something. He was completely caught off guard by what Sanders had said. He was sure that the former husband of Rebekah King was innocent. Detective Mahoney prided himself on being an excellent judge of people and he didn't believe for a second that the doctor was guilty. But what was this about a meeting between him and his ex-wife on the very night she was murdered? Did he miss something during his visit a few days ago? He gave it some thought and came to the conclusion that if Dr. Goldberg did murder his ex-wife then somehow or other managed to sneak into the open house, someone would have noticed. Even with all the drinking and merriment, someone would have seen him come in.

Even so, he knew that he had to make the trip back to Beverly Hills and find out more about this alleged meeting. He called to make sure that the doctor would be in before heading that way. He was told that he would need to be there by 9 a.m. sharp the next day, as the doctor would be going into surgery shortly thereafter. The receptionist hung up on him as soon as he agreed. Apparently, Mahoney had worn out his welcome.

He got up at the crack of dawn, poured himself a strong cup of coffee and managed to get on the road before 6:00 a.m. which was early enough to beat most of the traffic. He had made it clear, before being cut off that he needed at least 30 minutes of the doctor's time. He had also made it clear that it was urgent.

He hit some traffic due to an early morning accident near LAX but was still able to park the car two blocks from the doctor's office more than an hour before the scheduled meeting. He took a walk around the block a few times before going in.

The office door was locked when he arrived, but just a few minutes later a tall, skinny brunette with fashionable eyeglasses arrived to open up. She was just as pretty as the blonde receptionist from the other day, but not nearly as friendly. She gestured for him to sit down then went back to her paperwork. The doctor arrived just 20 minutes later looking rushed and not nearly as welcoming as he had the last time. He walked by Mahoney, nodded and then walked straight back to his office. Mahoney considered following him there uninvited, but at that very moment a call came through to the front desk and the receptionist told him that the doctor was ready to see him.

The doctor was reviewing a file when Mahoney walked in. Without looking up, the doctor told him to take a seat. He seemed preoccupied and not the same chatty doctor Mahoney had met just a few days prior. Mahoney sat down, placed his hands on the desk and without hesitation said, "You had dinner with Rebekah the night she was killed." It was a statement, not a question. The doctor looked up from his papers.

"Yes, I did," he said matter-of-factly.

"Don't you think that was important enough to tell me when I was here last time? You had dinner with your ex-wife on the very night she was murdered. In my book that ranks very high on the list of things that are important in a murder investigation." Mahoney crossed his arms and leaned back in his chair. He watched the doctor's expression, but there was no change in his demeanor.

"We had dinner that night because I was down in Dana Point for a meeting and I asked her if she wanted to meet me for a glass of wine and some tapas. I'll be honest and tell you that we had been talking once in a while over the past few months. It wasn't like I called her out of the blue." His voice sounded calm and confident and without even a touch of guilt. "But you're right, detective," he said rolling a pen around in his fingers. "It was something I should have mentioned." He raised his brows. "If I remember correctly, we ran out of time on our last meeting and I never got around to bringing it up. Besides, we met earlier in the day and I only stayed for one glass of wine as I had the long drive home. It must have just slipped my mind." He slapped his hand against his forehead indicating forgetfulness.

Mahoney took all this down before speaking. He looked up at Doctor Goldberg, made eye contact for a few seconds trying to decide if he believed him or not.

"How and why did you suddenly get back in touch with the woman who walked out on you several years ago? My understanding was that this chapter had been closed. Why now?" Mahoney asked, his eyes narrowly focused on the doctor. For a second a shadow passed over the face of the doctor making him look regretful. He lowered his eyes and sighed.

"I never got over her completely. That's the hard truth. I love my current wife and I have no regrets in marrying her, but part of me still misses Rebekah. She had a hold on me even though we hadn't spoken for," he paused for a second as searched his mind for how long it had been. "I don't know, five, maybe six years. *I* wanted to reconnect."

Mahoney gave the doctor a confused look. He knitted his brows and then asked, "Why? Why did you want to reconnect? Were you still attracted to her? Were there things that needed to be resolved?" The doctor shook his head.

"I just liked being with her. And yes, there were some things that weren't resolved. I still to this day have no idea why she left me." Mahoney wrote this down. He found the possible motive. The rich, successful doctor couldn't get over the fact that his wife had left him for no apparent reason.

"What was the name of the restaurant where you met her?" Mahoney asked trying to move on to establish his whereabouts. He may have had a motive, but there was still not a clear opportunity. The doctor thought for a second and then replied. "Café Valencia," he said. "I let Rebekah choose as I'm not as familiar with the places down in Orange County." Mahoney nodded and wrote down the name. He made a mental note to call the restaurant on his way home to verify this.

"Do you think someone would be able to confirm that you were there on that night?" The doctor thought about it and nodded.

"I guess so. I tend to be a good tipper, so maybe the waiter would know. I mean at my age and Rebekah's age I don't think we caused a stir, and it was over a week ago."

Mahoney nodded again. "We'll take care of that. They can always check credit card receipts. Do you remember what time you left the restaurant?"

"I do, actually." He lifted his arm to show the face of his watch. "I'm one of those people who always times things. I check the time on my watch when I get into the car and then again when I get out so I know how long it takes me door to door. And on that night I got into my car down in Dana Point at exactly 7:53 in the evening. I remember walking into my front door around 8:30." He stood up and stretched, "My wife can confirm that."

"Right," said Mahoney. "We will be contacting her shortly. That said, does your wife know that you were meeting your ex-wife for drinks and chit-chat?" Mahoney put down his notepad and gave him a hard stare. The doctor clasped his hands on the desk and looked down. *Apparently not,* thought Mahoney.

"She knew I had met with her a few times, but Sarah always thought it was about the divorce settlement. I wasn't completely honest with my wife. I told her that Rebekah was begging me for more money as a way to cover up the real reasons I had for meeting with her. I guess, in a sense, I was unfaithful to my current wife."

"Unfaithful? Did you sleep with her?"

Doctor Goldberg shook his head. "No, I never slept with her after our divorce, but meeting her for dinner and drinks and then lying to my wife is a form of infidelity. I should have been more up front with her. With Sarah, that is. Sarah isn't even the jealous type," he continued. "She would have been fine with our meetings if I had just told her the good old-fashioned truth." Mahoney nodded but didn't say anything. He understood how the doctor felt about meeting his ex-wife and then failing to tell his current wife. Technically, however, it wasn't cheating. The doctor picked up his cell and hit a speed dial button. A few seconds later someone picked up. "Sarah, darling," he said leaning back in his chair. "I have a detective here asking questions about that night I had dinner down in Orange County. Can you let him know when I got home that night?" There was a pause and he handed the phone to Mahoney.

The conversation lasted all of three minutes and he handed the phone back. "Sounds like it went exactly how you said it did. I suspect you'll have some explaining to do when you get home, but if she's not the jealous type it should go well." Mahoney tried to suppress a smile. He didn't know a single woman who would be nonplussed to hear that her husband was meeting an ex for drinks and dinner.

"I don't know why I kept it from her. She actually encouraged me to get in touch with her a few years after we married; She felt I needed closure. Maybe she worried that somewhere along the line, Rebekah would start causing problems. She was a difficult woman and became even more so later in life. Sarah had hoped that if I met with her a few times a year, she would leave us alone. But Sarah had no reason to be jealous of Rebekah. I adore my beautiful young wife and I have no feelings whatsoever for my ex." He hesitated for a second before adding. "I'm sorry that this happened to her, and hope they find the schmuck who did this, but I am relieved that the marriage is over."

Mahoney stood up and started for the door. "One more thing. I heard that there was a bitter argument right before you left the restaurant. Can you tell me anything about that?"

Keith Goldberg looked confused. He tilted his head to the side and said, "An argument? There wasn't an argument. She just told me she had to leave to get to this yoga party and I wanted to get on the road before it got too late and we said our goodnights. Who said there was an argument?"

Mahoney nodded. He believed the doctor was telling the truth.

Chapter 43

Mahoney left the doctor's office feeling confused. What was the motive? He had an airtight alibi, although with experience, he knew that spouses didn't always make the best alibis. He also knew there was probably more to the story than what the doctor told him, but from what he could see, the doctor seemed innocent. His desire to stay in touch with an ex-wife who left him suddenly with no warning seemed odd to Mahoney, but people put up with all sorts of things.

Mahoney made great time getting back to the office and arrived in time to find Sanders working away at his desk. Mahoney quietly leaned against the door and cleared his throat to get his partner's attention. "I don't think it was the doctor," he said when Sanders finally looked up and noticed his presence. "You know," he said sitting down on the one available chair. "I thought there might be blackmail or she had some goods on him that could ruin his career, but from what I see, he just wanted to stay in touch with her. Our highly successful doctor is a bit insecure." He laughed and shook his head in disbelief. "He just wanted closure, so he had regular dinner dates with his ex." He made a wide gesture with his hands expressing his disbelief. "Closure," he repeated. "Then all of his alibis check out. He did have dinner with Rebekah, he left the restaurant when he said he did, and he got home before the party got going. If he did drive back to kill her once the party was over, someone would have seen him. And that would also mean that our victim was the very last to leave." He looked closely at Sanders. "I can also say that I can sense a guilty man a mile away, and this guy did not act guilty. Unless he is a psychopath who can fool even the likes of me, he didn't do it. Oh and that argument you mentioned," he said waving his finger. "Never happened.

Sanders leaned back in his chair and placed his feet on the desk. "You sure about that? Getting rid of Rebekah would have been a big load off his mind. She was always going to be part of his scenery and she seemed capable of just about anything."

"Yeah, except in this case he didn't do it. He's not our suspect," Mahoney said with such finality that Sanders wasn't able come up with an argument. Mahoney had worked cases like this one many times before, and he had developed a keen sense of detecting culpability. Sanders wasn't quite there yet.

At that point there was a knock at the door. The only one who could knock that loudly and that insistently was Sue. Something was up. "Yes, Sue. Come on in." The door opened quickly, and sure enough, it was the sullen front desk clerk standing there. "Someone named Jessica Howard is waiting for you at the front desk. She said it was urgent." Both men sat up straight.

"Wonder why she's here?" asked Mahoney. "Did you two set up a date? What happened to the custom of the man picking her up at her place?"

Sanders stood up and shook his head. "Not funny, Mahoney. Something must be going on or else she would have called. Let's go see what she wants."

Mahoney nodded and said he would be there in a few minutes. He had something to clear up at his desk.

When Mahoney left his office exactly seven minutes later, he saw Sanders and Jessica huddled close together, near Sue's desk, which confirmed his suspicions. Sanders was interested in her and she seemed to reciprocate his feelings. Good for him. After his ego-busting marriage to that awful woman, he deserved someone better. Even though Mahoney never expressed much in the way of sympathy toward Sanders, he did feel some. Poor guy really got a rotten deal with that bitch of a wife. Everyone in the office – even grumpy Sue – was rooting for Sanders, hoping he would be able to find love again. James realized what an attractive couple Sanders and Jessica made, but then he pushed those thoughts aside and put his detective cap back on. She was obviously here for a reason other than to flirt with the younger detective. Whatever they were talking about it, looked serious.

"Good to see you, Jessica. I hope you've been well." He stood back a few feet from the two of them. Sanders gestured for him to come closer. "Hey. Mahoney. Come on over here. We have something important to tell you." Mahoney stepped next to Jessica and noticed she looked more tired than usual. There were dark circles under her eyes and her usual flawless complexion looked a bit dull. She was still lovely, but she looked exhausted. Sanders noticed him eyeing her and he gave him a look that spoke volumes.

"Jess has something to tell us," Sanders said not taking his eyes off the young woman.

"Here or in the office?" asked Mahoney as he started to back away and move towards the office.

"Right here," Sanders said. "Jess thinks she knows who the murderer is," he said quietly so as not to arouse too much attention. "Go ahead and tell him what you think."

She walked towards Mahoney and got so close, he thought she was about to plant a kiss on his cheek. Instead, she raised herself up on her toes and began to whisper in his ear. Sue watched from her desk. Jessica leaned right in and said, "I think I know who did it."

Chapter 44

The detectives gathered what they needed from their offices, made a few calls, and then got into their cars. Jessica decided to go back to the studio and call Detective Sanders later to follow up. She needed a nap or a strong cup of coffee, but there was too much going on now and she was running on pure adrenaline. She pulled a lightweight silk sweater over her shoulders, as there seemed to be a sudden chill in the air. She checked her reflection in the rearview mirror, applied a smear of light pink lip gloss and backed her car out of the parking lot. She would take a shower and fix herself up later. She needed to get to the studio and act like everything was normal, even though it was anything but. It would be busy when she got back, full of students eager to get to class and completely unaware of what was going on. Sometimes she wondered about these people who acted like yoga and or Pilates was the most important thing in their lives. It was a job for her and a job she liked, but there was more to life than exercise. But she had to put on her manager face and look like everything was and would always be okay even though it really wasn't.

It came to her early that morning as she rinsed out her coffee mug in her sink. She had a light breakfast of Naan toast with a touch of butter and her morning coffee. Her poor night's sleep was a result of a series of strange dreams that seemed to be delivering a message. One dream after another all with a similar theme. There was one in particular that struck a nerve. What was it about? Right before the alarm was to go off, she fell into a deep sleep and she knew that the dream had something to do with the murder. Ever since it had happened she had a nagging thought that she was missing something, but for the life of her she couldn't remember what it was. There was so much on her mind between the murder, running the studio, and trying to please everyone and anyone that it escaped her. She never had felt so sure about a message being delivered through a dream. Most of her dreams were just a fusion of frustrations and made little or no sense, but this one was different. She sat down next to Harry and began to rub behind his ears the way he liked it. A gentle calm filled her body and she closed her eyes trying to get her mind to focus. She took a few deep breaths and then it came to her.

The events at the open house had always been a blur, as she had been very busy trying to make sure everything went smoothly and that the current clientele was happy. It was also crucial that any potential new clientele had all the relevant information needed to convince them to join. Running here and there and making sure glasses were refilled and trays replenished, she had no time to see what was really going on. In her dream she saw the faces from the open house, and everyone was having a grand time. Except for one. It was foggy and unclear who this person was. Then the dream shifted to the Pilates studio, where Rebekah was sitting on a reformer. She was wearing a colorful cotton dress embellished with spaghetti straps. The dress was a swirl of bright summer colors and appeared to be incongruous with her mood. She looked to be very angry. Someone was with her hovering by her side, but she couldn't see who it was. The dream was very clear, but whoever was in the Pilates studio with her was just a figure. The rest of it was a blur of shapes and sizes and loud voices yelling and screaming. As she recalled the dream, she wrote it down in the journal she kept by the bed.

Then it came to her. She remembered what had happened on the night of the open house. As the party began to wind down and people started to make excuses for leaving early, she had noticed that Rebekah King was still hanging around seemingly having a good time. Jessica thought it was strange that she was still there, since most of the clients had already left and It was mostly teachers hanging around dancing to 80s music and having too much to drink. Jessica had been busy trying to get most of the studio cleaned up before the night crew came in to do a more thorough cleaning. She was anxious to get everyone out of there so she could lock up and go home and still get to bed at a decent time.

At one point, she noticed Declan stepping outside, with Rebekah following behind. She glanced out the front window and thought she saw them together in the parking lot. She couldn't tell if they were talking, arguing or going their separate ways. She went back to cleaning up and before too long, everyone had pretty much left. At that point, she decided to leave the rest of the clean up to the cleaning crew. She grabbed her cardigan and locked up. She got into her car as quickly as possible, just in case any strange men were hanging around the area. She drove home, went to bed, and forgot all about it. Now, between the dream and the memories, she realized that she knew it was Declan Stevens who murdered Rebecca King.

Chapter 45

Jessica told the two detectives exactly what she remembered and how she was able to remember. At first they were skeptical about her dream. Dreams rarely predicted the future, nor did they always accurately represent the past. Pinning a murder on someone based only on a dream was unheard of. However, in this case, the dream helped her to remember the course of events on that fateful evening. It didn't take long to get the ball rolling and to confront the man who had allegedly strangled Rebekah King in a Pilates studio on the very night they were having a party.

As Jessica focused on that night, things became more and more clear. She remembered something that was crucial in solving the case. The night of the murder, as she stayed behind picking up plastic glasses half full of wine and throwing away trays of broken crackers and stale veggies, she thought she heard some yelling from outside in the parking lot. She glanced out the front door, thinking it was probably just a few drunks arguing about something or other. As she stepped away from the window, she thought she had seen Declan Stevens standing in the middle of the parking lot, holding onto the arm of a woman. The woman was wearing a form-fitting cotton summer dress with spaghetti straps. At that time, she figured it was one of his many female friends and she let it go. It was only after the dream that she put it all together. The dress belonged to Rebekah King, and she was clearly in an altercation with Declan. As the memories came rushing in, she was able to relay to the detectives everything she had seen that night. It all made sense. Declan Stevens had murdered Rebekah King.

Mahoney called it in and two squad cars were sent out immediately. He and Sanders followed behind them. They arrived in less than 13 minutes, finding Stevens meditating on a large silk pillow in his living room. He didn't seem surprised to see them arrive at the door, as if he had known deep down, this moment would have come sooner or later. He offered no resistance at all and listened carefully as they read him his rights. They took him away in cuffs and he waved at the woman who had been gardening the day before and apparently owned the property. She watched and said nothing.

Mahoney was curious about the motive for the crime. He had his doubts about the dashing yoga instructor from the get-go, but he never pegged him as a murderer, a phony, a ladies' man, maybe even a narcissist, but never a killer. The jury would have to decide on that.

He said very little as they escorted him out the door. He kept his gaze low, not making eye contact with the detectives. Just days ago, Sanders had been sitting in Steven's bungalow, convinced that this relatively young yoga teacher was incapable of murder.

Later on, as the details were revealed, the detectives learned more about what had allegedly happened that night of the murder.

Several nights before the evening of her death, Rebekah and Declan met up for drinks in a place they had discovered where they knew they could be discreet. Neither of them wanted to run into anyone from the studio, as it wouldn't bode well for them if word got out they were seeing each other. It was a small, cozy bar on a side street off of PCH in Corona Del Mar. That night, Declan was in the mood for sex, and he expected Rebekah to feel the same way. After all, their usual pattern was two or three drinks followed by some passionate sex at his place, which wasn't far from the bar. This time, however, Rebekah was in no mood for a night of passion. She was tense, angry and extremely critical of him, which, was a side of Rebekah he'd never seen. Stevens had his pick of women, but he was starting to really enjoy his time with Rebekah. She had a confidence about her that was rare among younger women. The sex was great, and he had no intentions of letting that go. He had never felt the sting of rejection either. Not since high school when his height and movie star good looks made him the most desirable boy in his class.

That evening she had made it clear that whatever it was they had, it was over. She was having financial problems and needed to move on. All that yoga and peaceful meditation did little or nothing to control his temper after she made it clear that she was dumping him. As the story unfolded, he felt he had been pursued by Rebekah and, in time, he had fallen for her. He had always figured that eventually he would tire of her and move on, but he'd no idea that it would be her decision to end things. Just like that, the sweet, funny and imminently sexy woman became a monster. She threatened to expose him to the studio and insist he get fired for sexual harassment.

On the night of the open house she was adamant that she wanted nothing more to do with him. He figured that after that night in the bar where she made it clear that she was no longer interested in him as a lover, she would crawl back begging him for forgiveness. He decided he would then end things with her once and for all. That way he would be the one to do the dumping. They left the party, being careful that no one would notice them leaving together, and began to argue in the parking lot. Rebekah slapped him in the face and he grabbed her arm. This was what Jessica had seen that night. Then they kissed and made up. The show of force was a real turn on for Declan and he liked the fact they were outside in an open parking lot. Yet such open displays of affection were not Rebekah's thing - at least not then. He tried to get her into the car, where he hoped to have sex with her. The thought if it made him delirious with desire. She refused to get in.

By then, everyone had left the party, and Declan led Rebekah by the hand up the long staircase. She came willingly, despite her earlier refusal to get in the car. He pulled out a key from his pocket. Since he was sometimes the last one to teach in the evenings, he kept a front door key so he could close up at the end of the workday. He looked at her dressed in a tight-fitting summer beach dress with strappy red sandals and her hair pulled expertly into a messy bun. She was not beautiful the way so many women at the studio were beautiful, but her sex appeal was overpowering. He could feel a raging hard-on under his khaki trousers and at that moment, he wanted her more than anything. Between the champagne, the pot he had smoked earlier and her feisty demeanor, he was ready to carry her up those stairs and screw her blind.

She went up the stairs with him happily. They couldn't keep their hands off each other as they tried to climb the steep stairs. She whispered in his ear that she wanted him to ravage her in the studio; It was something she often fantasized about.

She grabbed his hand and pulled him along towards the back. When they got into the Pilates studio, he pinned her against the front wall pulling up her dress then pulling down her lacy black panties so she could mount him. As soon as she climbed on top and he entered her, the barrage of insults began. He was a low life, a shitty lover and a loser. She never felt any attraction to him and she was with him out of sheer boredom. His huge hard-on suddenly went soft. This, more than anything, infuriated him. It was too much. He knew she liked rough sex, so he thought maybe this was her way of introducing some foreplay into this already sick relationship and he played along with her. He held her down and pressed himself against her slender body. He could feel she was struggling to breathe but the intensity of her anger turned him on. She resisted and continued with the insults, which were starting to get tiresome. He then grabbed her neck and began to choke the air out of her. She resisted and it triggered something ugly inside him. He felt a deep hatred for her unlike anything he had ever felt before. For several minutes, he kept his strong hands around her neck until all the air was choked out of her. Her body went limp and he realized what he had done. He spent a good hour cleaning up any traces of evidence and left a bit of a mess behind for no particular reason other than he thought it would increase the number of potential suspects. He wiped away the fingerprints from the studio, and then left, locking the door behind him.

Chapter 46

Now it was up to a defense attorney to represent Stevens and the jury to decide whether or not he was guilty. He had a bail hearing in a few days, but for Mahoney and Sanders, the case was over.

Once it was officially over and they had their guy, detective Sanders called Jessica to thank her for all her help. He didn't have to call her, nor did he usually call witnesses once a case was resolved, but he wanted to. He didn't want to lose touch, but he also wasn't sure how she felt about things.

Jessica was glad to hear from him. She was actually very glad. After the mystery had been solved, she realized that maybe it was time to make some big changes in her life. It was as if she was holding her breath the entire length of the investigation. It made her realize that the studio no longer held any magic for her, and it was time to do something else. Once she was able to take a deep breath, she knew it was time to go. Work was as busy as ever, if not more so. The phone was ringing non-stop, and an influx of new clients were anxious to join the studio where a real murder had taken place. The television drama show 48 Hours was planning to do a story on the murder and everyone secretly hoped they could be there during filming. Jessica, on the other hand, had different plans.

After thinking it over, she went home, made arrangements with her favorite dog sitter, called Spencer to give him the news and then she packed her bags. Spencer begged her to rethink her departure, but her mind was made up. They would find someone else to replace her and, within weeks, she'd be just a vague memory. People come and go.

She planned to drive up the California coast, starting in Santa Barbara, then driving north through San Luis Obispo, finishing up in the Bay area where she had a few college friends. She needed a full week to unwind and leave the brutal case behind. It had been less than ten days since she got the early morning call from Monica Gallagher, but it seemed like a lifetime.

She threw her bags into the trunk of her car and started up her phone GPS. She knew the way – it was easy – but she wanted to avoid any traffic, if possible. Just as she was pulling out, her phone rang. She didn't recognize the number but answered anyway. "Hello," she said, deciding to take a chance. Usually it was some silly caller trying to sell her something or tell her she was wanted by the FBI. This time, however, the number looked legitimate.

"Hey, It's Martin Sanders. I'm using my personal cell to contact you."

"Oh," she replied, feeling a flutter in her heart at hearing his voice. Over the past few days she found herself thinking about him more and more. There was something eminently sexy about him, but up until now he had been just the man trying to solve a murder mystery. It had been a long time since a man could have that effect on her and she was enjoying the butterflies in her belly. "Hi, Martin," she said. "What can I do for you?" She was driving away from her condo and heading toward the road that would take her to the 405 freeway towards Santa Monica, where she would cut over via the 10 freeway to take the scenic route up the coast.

"I'm just checking in to see how you're doing and if maybe..." He hesitated, losing his nerve for a second. He wasn't sure if he was barking up the wrong tree by asking her out. She was a beautiful young woman who probably had a line of men out the door waiting to go out with her. He might not stand a chance, but it was at least worth a try. He had noticed how she sometimes looked at him and it gave him enough confidence to ask her out. The worst that could happen would be that she'd say no, and he'd let it go.

"Well," she said as she pulled into some early afternoon traffic. "I'm heading up the coast for a few days to get away, but I will be back next week. How does next Friday sound to get together?" The sun was melting yellow and orange along the Pacific Ocean as she drove past Crystal Cove State Park. She loved Southern California, but it was time to get away and see something new. A change of scenery, rugged hiking along the cliffs of Montana del Oro, wine tasting and visiting a few old friends would be exactly what she needed to get over the past ten days. She felt light, free and as happy as she had felt in a very long time.

"Next Friday sounds perfect," he said. "It's a date."

"Sounds absolutely delightful," she said meaning every word. "I am looking forward to seeing you when I get back."

Chapter 47

James Mahoney decided to take the next day off and spend it with his wife. She had the entire day off and they needed to spend some quality time together. He had worked on harder cases, but none that seemed so draining as this one had been. Maybe it was just his age, but he had no plans to retire anytime soon. Lizzie knew enough not to ask him about it, but when he told her they caught their man, she was thrilled. "I knew you would eventually. You always do."

He told her they would sleep late (which, for him, meant until 7 a.m.) and then have their morning coffee before heading to the beach for a long morning walk. They would stop at a beachside restaurant for a late lunch and then come home for a long nap. Mahoney was looking forward to spending the time with Lizzie and getting some much-needed rest. He was exhausted from this case, but still had the energy to blow off some steam. What better way than a lovely beach morning with his wife.

Lizzie had been working long hours at the hospital and fatigue was starting to show on her face. There were darkish circles around her lovely green eyes, and they had lost their shine. A day away from the hospital was exactly what she needed to feel like herself again.

"So, "she asked as she grabbed the beach umbrella from the garage. "Are you happy now that the case is over?" She gestured for him to open the trunk of the car so she could put the umbrella and beach towels inside. Her hair was pulled back into a ponytail and she had on a yellow cap that she bought during their trip two years ago to the Grand Canyon.

"Let's just say I'm glad it's all over. These past couple of weeks have been really rough, and to be honest with you, until the very last minute we didn't have any solid leads." He helped her shove all the beach paraphernalia into the car. "Let's go and get us some good clean ocean air. That's why we live here isn't it?" She smiled and shrugged. A nice day at the beach sounded just perfect.

About the Author

D.J. Swiger is a writer, linguist and Pilates instructor living in Southern California. D.J. Swiger is originally from New York but has lived and traveled all over the world. In addition to writing and learning new languages, she loves teaching Pilates, hiking and reading as many books as possible.

Made in the USA
Monee, IL
23 February 2021